BAYOU MAGIC

Jewell Parker Rhodes

LITTLE, BROWN AND COMPANY
New York Boston

Little, Brown and Company

Hachette Book Group
1290 Avenue of the Americas, New York, NY 10104
Visit us at lb-kids.com

Little, Brown and Company is a division of Hachette Book Group, Inc.
The Little, Brown name and logo are trademarks of Hachette Book Group, Inc.

The publisher is not responsible for websites (or their content) that are not owned by the publisher.

First Edition: May 2015

Library of Congress Cataloging-in-Publication Data

Rhodes, Jewell Parker.
  Bayou magic / by Jewell Parker Rhodes.—First edition.
    pages cm
  Summary: Visiting her grandmother in the Louisiana bayou, ten-year-old Maddy begins to realize that she may be the only sibling to carry on the gift of her family's magical legacy.
  ISBN 978-0-316-22484-0 (hardcover)—ISBN 978-0-316-22486-4 (ebook)—ISBN 978-0-316-36456-0 (library edition ebook) [1. Bayous—Fiction. 2. Magic—Fiction. 3. Grandmothers—Fiction. 4. African Americans—Fiction. 5. Louisiana—Fiction.] I. Title.
  PZ7.R3476235Bay 2015
  [Fic]—dc23

2014029152

10 9 8 7 6 5 4 3 2 1

RRD-C

Printed in the United States of America

BAYOU MAGIC

Dedicated to the wonderful
students of Flint Hill School

New Orleans

My name is Madison Isabelle Lavalier Johnson. Maddy, for short.

I live in New Orleans. I have four sisters. I'm the youngest, almost ten. I'm the littlest, too. "Bird bones," Ma gently teases, pinching my wrist. But she knows I'm strong.

All Lavalier women are strong.

"We're a stew," says Ma. "African. French. Native and Spanish blood, too."

It's Saturday. Me and Ma are in the kitchen making jambalaya. I like to cook. My sisters don't.

Ma slices onions. I clean shrimp.

"The whole world is kin, Maddy. Blood flows like river water."

I snap, slip off pink shells.

"I'm going to miss you, Maddy." Ma kisses my cheek.

"I'll miss you, too," I say, trembling, scared to visit Ma's momma, my mysterious Grandmère.

Last four summers, a different sister has visited Grandmère.

Aisha says, "The bayou's boring. No TV."

Dionne says, "Grandmère's mean. Makes you clean dishes, but better not sweep a spider's web!"

"No microwave. Only a stinky outhouse," says Aisha, wrinkling her nose.

Layla shudders, poses dramatically. "Don't tell Ma I said—Grandmère's weird. She sleepwalks. Tells the craziest tales."

"Think slithering ghosts," says Aleta. "Think howls. Think creatures gobbling, crunching your fingers and toes. Bugs laying eggs in your ear."

"Shadows," groans Layla. "Everywhere. Coming alive, diving through the window, falling on your bed."

"Boo!" says Aleta, making me jump.

~

Grandmère Lavalier doesn't have a telephone. Four times she's mailed us an envelope holding a piece of brown paper with a name scratched like bent chicken wire.

Yesterday, Ma opened a letter and paper fluttered to the floor. I picked it up.

MADISON

Maddy. Me.

Even though I was expecting it, I couldn't stop staring at my name. My turn to have a bayou summer.

My turn to stay with Grandmère, who only visited New Orleans on the days my sisters and I were born.

"Once Momma saw you were healthy," Ma says,

"she went back to the bayou. Said she couldn't stand the city. Couldn't breathe the stale air.

"Momma hasn't left the bayou since you were born."

I pressed the paper, MADISON, to my chest, trying to quiet my heart.

My sisters cluck-clucked, patted my back. "Too bad," said Dionne, woeful. "No malls. No burgers."

"Glad it's not me," quipped Layla, her beaded cornrows clacking as she shook her head. Aisha, the oldest, sniffed, "I'll write." But I know she won't.

Aleta, the next youngest, the one who teases me most, gripped my hand. "I'll never forget you. If you don't make it back, if the swamp swallows you, if you're lost in the wild . . ."

"Shoo," said Ma.

But the damage was done. I crumpled the paper and hid it inside a sock in my drawer.

Dionne, Aleta, and Layla want to be just like Aisha. She's fourteen, popular, and pretty. Whatever Aisha does, they want to do, too.

I prefer listening, watching, dreaming. Sometimes my dreams come true. Last winter I dreamed about a boy who could fly. Without asking, Pa gave me *Peter Pan*. Ma gave me Miss Hamilton's *The People Could Fly*. Imagine, slaves becoming birds, flying back to Africa.

Mostly, I don't remember my dreams. Aisha says she can tell when I've been dreaming. "You're bug-eyed in the morning. Got sweat on your upper lip."

This morning, I lick away that sweat. Aisha sees me. Not knocking, she barges right into the bathroom.

I squeeze paste on my toothbrush and move away from the mirror so Aisha can fix her hair. She combs it to one side, swipes pink gloss across her lips.

Making tiny circles, I clean my teeth.

"Grandmère's a witch," she says, staring at me in the mirror. Snapping her fingers, she flounces from the room.

Wait. A witch? Really?

~

"Time to sauté."

I grab the cast-iron pot. Pour in golden oil. Ma adds onions. I add chopped celery, green peppers.

Tomorrow, I leave.

I murmur, "Do I have to? Do I have to go? Visit Grandmère?"

"Your Grandmère would be unhappy if you didn't go."

"Would you? Be unhappy?"

Ma doesn't answer, just strokes my hair.

With a wooden spoon, Ma stirs. The onions turn silky brown, the celery softens, and the peppers wilt. The savory smell comforts me.

Quiet is the best part of cooking. Me and Ma watching the stew blend.

Today, though, my mind won't still.

I add spices. Garlic. Bay leaf. Hot sauce. Worcestershire.

"Don't measure—cook with your heart," Ma teaches.

I lift the bag of rice and pour. Just enough rice to

layer the pot's bottom. Then I add chicken stock Ma made from bones from Sunday's roasted chicken. Rice and vegetables float, the bay leaf twirls. I make a good jambalaya.

"Don't worry," Ma says, her voice mellow and high-pitched. "You're not your sisters."

Nervous, I clench my hands.

"Every stew is different, Maddy. Special. Put the lid on."

I turn down the fire. Blue flames sputter and glow. Me and Ma stand side by side, staring at the simmering broth beneath the glass top.

"Momma taught me how to make this stew. Now I've taught you."

Ma kneels, surprising me. She hugs me quick, strong, and tight. She pulls back. "Oh, Maddy, I wish I could go, too."

Looking into her gray-green eyes, I see myself, reflected. Brown curls. Brown skin.

I'm swimming in Ma's eyes. Ma has happy tears.

My reflection flickers, shimmers.

Trust your heart, I hear, echoing inside me. Like Ma's speaking beneath water.

Lightning shoots through me. I exhale, my body tingling. I see myself... *on a shore—a full moon high, mirrored in blue-black waters.*

It's going to be fine, I hear myself say.

More than fine, Ma's voice again. *You're you.*

Then I'm jolted back. Ma stands, adds shrimp to the pot. I blink.

Something's different. I feel it. I look about. The clock shaped like a birdhouse chimes two o'clock. The cabinets are a dull white. The linoleum is still cracked, the window screen torn. Our kitchen is small, barely enough room for the stove, the fat refrigerator, and the sink. For Ma and me.

Tomorrow I'll be gone. I feel warm, a burning wick glowing inside me.

"Do you really wish you could go?" I ask Ma.

She smiles, sadly, sweet.

For the first time ever, I'm doing something Ma wishes she could do.

Be me. Be young. Visit Grandmère.

Over the Hill, Through the Woods

Louisiana doesn't have any hills. It's flatter than a pancake, and it doesn't have woods with snowy pines.

It's below sea level, so water kisses and hugs the dirt, making swamps and wetlands. It's always warm or warmer. Hot or hotter.

As we drive, road signs—GAS, FOOD, LODGING— become fewer. I see more trucks. Motorcycle riders with paisley bandannas wave to me. Yellow road signs show black deer leaping. Seventy miles gone; sixty miles left to go.

Driving to Grandmère's house, I feel like I'm traveling to a foreign land. I'm used to the city. Concrete, brick, and steel. In school, we study nature—read books, take field trips to the Audubon Zoo, the Audubon Butterfly Garden, Insectarium, and Aquarium of the Americas. I like the gift shops. I buy magnets to remind me of what I've seen—turtles in the aquarium; an alligator in the zoo; and honeybees, the state bug, living in glass-walled hives.

The Mississippi is supposed to be wild, but I've only ever seen the river chained by levees to make waterways for tugboats, steamboats, and cargo ships. When Katrina hit, they said, "Water became dangerous, spilling into homes." I was only five. We Johnsons went to Baton Rouge.

When we came back, the river was tame. Flat, boring.

Traveling deep into the country, the world seems huge. Miles and miles of open space. No high-rise buildings, trees so old and big dinosaurs might've chewed them. The sky is crayon-streaked—yellow, orange, and purple with marshmallow clouds.

Ma says nothing. Just drives, with the windows down, wind whistling through the car. Static scratches when I turn the radio dial. Tires *slap-slap, slap-slap*, pounding "*...to Grandmère's house, to Grandmère's house we go.*"

I'm still scared, but somehow excited, too.

Leaving home, my sisters expected me to cry. I didn't. My eyes stayed dry.

Now I breathe wet, salty air. Farther south, there's a lot more water. Rivers, streams, swamps. The Gulf of Mexico.

The sun is high. Bright. Hotter than a smoke pit.

Sweating, my dress sticks to my legs. My legs stick to the seat. I'm drenched.

A bird screeches.

My head tilts sideways. Trees, sky, and clouds steadily zoom by. The sun lowers toward ground.

I blink. So hot. *Slap-slap, slap-slap* beat the tires. Sweat weighs me down. Wind whizzes, warbles. Gentle rumblings and heat lull.

I look left. Ma studies the road.

I look right.

A firefly sits, blinking on the rim of the car door.

I keep still. It's beautiful. Its body, brown-striped, shaped like a sunflower seed; its wings, fragile, flapping. The firefly turns its itty-bitty head. Black pindrop eyes watch me. I watch back.

Its stomach sparkles yellow-green. *It's a signal*, I think. But for what?

Holding my breath, I swear I can hear its heart beating.

"We're here."

Ma shakes me. Was I dreaming?

Tires crunch pebbles and dirt. I rub my cheek, which is creased from the ridges on the seat. The car bounces, jerks.

Headlights brighten a square house on stilts. Above it rises a crescent moon.

"There's my momma," Ma says, proud. "Your Grandmère."

I don't see anyone.

The shack, gray, dried wood, looks like it's floating. The roof is tin, sparkling, reflecting moonlight. Its window eyes are lit with candles like a carved pumpkin.

I hold back, don't unclick my seat belt. I want to go home. Back to New Orleans.

"Come on, Maddy."

I stay in the car.

A match flickers. A shadow holding high a kerosene lamp separates from a post on the porch.

I swallow a yelp, then exhale. "She's tiny!"

I imagined Grandmère was a GIANT. Instead, she's barely bigger than me, wearing baggy overalls that make her seem even smaller. But her shadow is long. It stretches, spills down the steps, reaching toward me.

"Be polite," says Ma.

I get out of the car. There're no other houses or stores in sight. No streetlights. No one else around—just me, Ma, and Grandmère—deep in the dark bayou.

Grandmère's face, expressionless, appears out of

the shadows of the porch. She has high cheekbones. Piercing eyes.

"I want to go home."

"Hush," Ma says, pushing me forward.

I walk, my Sunday dress swishing at my knees. Dirt, pebbles, sticks scratch my shoes. I don't look in Grandmère's eyes. Instead, I stare at her bright-white, curly hair, luminous like the moon.

I shudder, feeling like she can see deep inside me.

Ma squeezes my shoulder.

There's quiet all around, stillness in the lush green trees. Silent stars and sky. Moths dance about the kerosene light.

Grandmère squints and asks, "Did my firefly come?"

I'm confused. People don't own fireflies. Do they?

Standing tall on the shadowy porch, gazing down at me, Grandmère waits, like my answer is the most important thing in the world.

I nod.

Grandmère's hands clap. "A good sign."

"Ma, I don't understand."

"You're your Grandmère's child," Ma says, wistful, proud, confusing me more.

I tremble. A warm breeze washes over me. But there isn't any wind. The bayou air is thick, heavy. Draped about me like a shawl.

Grandmère sets down the lamp. Her arms reach for me. I feel an urge—ever so deep, pushing, pulling me.

I walk up the porch steps, then hesitate.

Grandmère reaches for me, hugging me tight. She smells of Creole flavors—celery, onion, and green pepper.

A firefly lights on the porch rail, its wings black, glittering.

I feel the warmth of Grandmère's body, the beating of her heart, her breath in my ear.

"You'll have to be strong."

Words so soft, I'm not sure I hear. I don't know what they mean. But I *feel* a deep sadness. Trembling, I twist out of Grandmère's arms.

She stares, sizing me up.

I look, over my shoulder, at Ma. She's smiling, happy. She doesn't sense Grandmère's sadness.

I look at Grandmère. She nods like we've agreed upon something. Made a pact.

"About time you got here, Maddy. The bayou and me, we've been waiting. Been dreaming about you forever."

Dewberries

I wake, disoriented. Off-kilter.

Where am I?

Then I remember. After dinner, Ma and Grandmère in the rockers, me on the steps, we sat quiet on the porch, watching the bayou like we were watching TV.

Grandmère kept saying, "I've never lived anywhere else but here." Each time I heard her, I'd marvel more at how velvet moss covered bark. How silvery willow-tree branches hung, forming canopies. How moths tried to kiss the blue flame inside the lamp. How right off Grandmère's front stoop was the most beautiful and frightening world I'd ever seen.

I kissed Ma when she left. I bit my tongue—still scared. Still trying to be brave, but wanting to beg her not to go.

Grandmère tucked me in bed, tight with a crisp white sheet.

"You know how to listen quiet."

I felt like I'd passed a test.

~

Waking, I stretch my arms and toes. Ripples of silver tin shape the ceiling. In between ridges, there are spiderwebs. I almost scream.

I pull my legs up, tight. I feel itchy. Creepy.

I don't see any spiders. Just webs. Like lace. Delicate connecting threads filling the ceiling's hollows.

If spiders don't bite me, I think I'll be fine.

I like how the cot holds me. It's snug. But there's no door. Just a sheet on a rope making a screen.

There are no stuffed animals or a closet of frilly dresses. No twin beds. No electric ceiling lights.

I hear Grandmère shuffling, trying not to clang pots and pans.

For a moment, I feel good. Like I was meant to wake up here, feeling sunlight streaking through the window above my head.

Grandmère's house isn't fancy. Just logs and wood slats. Mesh for windows. *Grandmère's poor,* my sisters probably thought.

But I feel like I'm in a storybook, in a magical cottage deep in the forest.

Still, I can't help but remember Aisha's warning: "A witch." *A witch's house?* I try to calm myself.

～

I smell bacon and something else, tangy and sweet. Dewberries. My stomach rumbles.

"I'm awake."

"There's a shirt, overalls at the foot of your bed." Grandmère's voice comes from the other side of the screen. She starts to hum.

I hum, too. Grandmère stops. I stop.

She hums again, low and deep. I match her pitch, only higher. She hums another note. I hum it back. Separated by the sheet, it feels like a game.

Grandmère hums another note, then another and another. A repeating pattern. I follow her lead. Our voices mingle, making a happy tune.

With back and front pockets, my overalls are just like hers, only smaller. I've never had overalls before, just my sisters' hand-me-down skirts, dresses. I like the pockets.

I slide the hanging sheet.

Grandmère quiets like a spell's been broken.

I see the small kitchen. I see Grandmère's cot, covered by a quilt with a pattern of blue and white fish. There are wildflowers by the window. Not a single mirror. Another reason why my sisters didn't like it here.

Grandmère's wrinkles are deep. Her hands are covered with brown spots. She looks like Ma, except older, an elderly sprite. Tinier, too. Bird-boned like me.

"You done studying me?"

I swallow. I don't want Grandmère to think I'm rude.

"There's better studying to do than studying me," she challenges.

"Like what?"

"Like how these dewberries here, plus some sugar," she says, pouring brown crystals, "make syrup. Perfect for griddle cakes."

On the stove, there are no gas or electric coils, just red-gray coals on a shelf beneath the pot.

"Can I help?"

"You cook?"

"Yes, ma'am. Ma taught me everything you taught her."

"Did she now?" Grandmère's eyes shine.

I've passed another test.

"Get some eggs. From Sweet Pea."

"Who?"

Grandmère laughs, sounding like sparkling water over rock. I don't feel embarrassed; it's a happy laugh.

"Sweet Pea. My chick. Her coop is 'round back."

I dash out the door, leaping off the porch. I've never seen a live chicken. Stones and pressed dirt make a trail leading past a garden to a yellow-painted box, low and long.

Sweet Pea is beautiful—reddish brown, with copper silk feathers. A red crown, a yellow beak. She cocks her head. Her right eye, a black pupil surrounded by hazel, blinks. Or winks?

I tiptoe forward. Sweet Pea sits on a shelf. Wood chips line the floor. She looks at me.

Do chickens smile?

Sweet Pea stands on her two three-toed feet. Beautiful brown eggs nestle in hay.

She's proud. Her feathers are puffed; her beak pecks forward and back, then down. She's inviting me.

I walk, slowly. Softly. Crunching dirt.

I lift each egg, warm, smooth. I cradle two of them. Miss Sweet Pea clacks, her beak jutting, like she's asking for something.

"Thank you?" I try.

Miss Sweet Pea clucks, turns in a circle and lifts

her feet, one by one, and then, shimmying her feathers, sits again.

Grandmère is in the kitchen flipping meal cakes.

Without turning, she says, "Bring the eggs here."

"How'd you know I'm here?"

"Know plenty." Grandmère cracks the eggs, and I watch as they sizzle, the whites turning opaque then bright white and the yolk becoming a firmer, quivering yellow.

"Do you know Sweet Pea talks?"

Brows arched, Grandmère stares at me.

"I mean, not words," I say nervously. "But she wanted me to speak. Say 'Thank you,' I think. So I did."

"So you should," says Grandmère, turning back to the stove. "Being ungrateful is the worst."

I slip into the chair, ready to eat.

"Wash your hands."

I mumble-grumble.

"*Non*, no. Don't have eyes in the back of my head."

"How'd you know what I was saying?"

"Mumbling, you mean?"

"Sorry."

" 'Sorry' accepted."

I worry Grandmère's mad. Back home, at least once a day, my sisters are mad at me.

Smiling, Grandmère flips an egg, not mad at all. "Ask the firefly, Maddy. Miss Firefly knows how I know. All kinds of knowing, all different ways to know."

My sisters are right. Grandmère *is* strange. But if she's strange, then I'm strange, too. It's daylight and I'm looking for a glowing bug.

"Is it here? The firefly?"

"Down by the riverside," Grandmère says. "Not 'it,' *she*. Won't see her 'til night."

She points to a water-filled ceramic bowl. Beside it is a soap bar with green specks.

Before I ask, Grandmère answers, "Thyme. For strength, courage."

"I didn't know that."

"Lots you don't know."

I scrub my hands, arms. Even my face. "Me and Ma cook with thyme." I dry myself, smelling lemony, woodsy. I feel better already.

Today, Grandmère breaks the quiet, her voice warm. "Rituals are important."

"What's a ritual?" I bite a piece of bacon.

"Doing something the same way every day."

I nod, munching. Four days here and I'm less scared. It helps knowing how I'm going to start the day. "Dishes next."

I wash. Grandmère dries.

Then, we sit on the porch—Grandmère on the rocker, me on the step.

We sit watching birds fly, lizards zigzag through dirt. I study leaves—three-point leaves, one-point leaves, and leaves with smooth or jagged edges. Leaves have veins that don't carry blood, only moisture.

We read the bayou like Pa reads his newspaper.

The bayou brings good news to me. But seeing shadows floating, quivering on the ground, seeing branches sway, bend, and snap, I sense there could be bad news, too. How else to explain weeping willows? Or how a pretty, sparkly snake with dark bands and a red stripe can be a rattler?

"Canebrake rattler," I remember Grandmère saying. "Tries to pretend it's sweet."

The bayou excites me, but I haven't left the yard. Grandmère excites me, too. But sometimes she frowns, and I sense the unhappiness I felt when I first hugged her.

"Bored, Maddy?"

"No, ma'am."

Grandmère stands and comes to sit beside me. We're both tiny, like two little kids on a step, but Grandmère is wrinkled all over. Her right hand trembles. Her eyes are the softest brown.

I shiver a little. Grandmère is looking inside me, seeing me from the inside out. Like she knows everything about me. Even stuff I don't know.

I want to blurt, "Are you a witch?" Instead I ask, "Is this how Ma lived?"

"Oui. She outgrew it—will you?"

I squirm, not ready to answer. "In stories," I say, "characters never outgrow magic lands."

"Is this what you think this is? Magic?"

"Yes. No." I wiggle my feet. "Maybe."

Grandmère laughs.

I'm flustered.

"Let's work."

This is when the day changes. When I feel Grandmère's most testing me. It's like a teacher saving up a hard question, asking just me, "Maddy, do you know the answer?"

Sometimes I do, sometimes I don't.

But I also know that Grandmère seems to be asking me questions without really asking. It's like there's a secret between us. But I don't know what it is any more than I know why Grandmère sometimes seems so sad.

"Grandmère, what's our work today?"

"Herbs. Bark. Picking what's good for ailments. Healing the sick."

"Isn't there a drugstore?"

"Me, I'm the drugstore."

I blush, feeling dumb. I knew there weren't any stores.

Grandmère pretends not to notice. "Old days

there weren't any drugstores. Doctors, either. Folks made do. Lavaliers been healing for over two hundred years. What do you think of that, Maddy-girl?"

I lick my lips. I can hear the dare. "Show me."

"Come on," she says, handing me a basket from beneath the porch.

Together, we search the yard, the garden's herb patch. A beat and a step behind, I do whatever Grandmère does. We dig in the dirt and pluck green and brown stems.

"Always good things at the base of trees."

I nod, agreeing, like I know what Grandmère's talking about.

"This here, elderberry." She plucks.

I twirl the stem; tiny white flowers spin.

"The flower is good for fever. Headaches."

I squat. "What's that?"

"Baby's breath."

I scoot left, touching a tree with three-point leaves. "Oooh, I know what this is. Ma showed me a picture. It's . . . it's—"

"Sassafras."

I sing, "Sip it in the morning, sip it in the evening. I like sassafras. You like sassafras. We like sassafras tea!"

"You sing good, Maddy."

"Thanks." But I feel silly. "Ma said sassafras calms."

"Did she now?"

"I was nervous before a test. She didn't have sassafras tea, so she taught me the song. Ma says, 'City dirt doesn't grow sassafras.'"

"Bayou has plenty. Sassafras, good for bruises. Make a paste and bruises heal quick."

I sniff the bark, chew a tiny piece.

"What's it taste like?"

"Root beer."

Grandmère laughs, strokes my hair. "You remind me of me."

"That's good, isn't it?"

"Depends."

My face twists. I don't understand. Ma's always flattered when someone says I act, talk, or look like her.

I pluck sassafras bark, laying it in the basket.

Shade fills the trees. The sun is going down. It's always this way—time slows when me and Grand-mère sit on the porch, then it flies like lightning when we're working.

We walk back to the cottage.

"This bayou's been the Lavaliers' home for generations. After slavery, all kinds of folks lived here."

"I know," I say, skipping. "French, Africans, some Spanish, and native peoples, too."

"Everybody helped one another."

"Made a community," I recite. "Everybody was either friend or kin. Blood like river water flows."

"Who told you that?"

"Ma."

Grandmère opens the screen door. It's not any cooler inside. Sweat drips down my neck.

"Your ma's strong. She remembers our stories."

"I'm strong."

I want Grandmère to say, *Yes, you are, Maddy-girl.* But all she says is, "Make me some sassafras tea."

Grandmère's changing moods make me nervous. I scratch a match to light the stove. I fill the kettle.

Water drains over the bark. I hope it calms Grandmère.

I pour steaming water over the bark and let it steep.

"Maddy, who do you want to be when you grow up?"

She didn't ask "what." *What do you want to be?* I know the safe answer to that. Answer "doctor," "lawyer," "engineer," "businesswoman," and everyone smiles. But grown-ups, except for Grandmère, never, ever ask *who*.

Who do you want to be?

Strangely, I feel like I can tell Grandmère things I can't tell Ma.

"A hero. Like in my stories," I rush. "I want to do good. Be brave." I stop, embarrassed.

Grandmère gazes at me, curious. "To be a hero, bad things have to happen."

I don't want bad things happening.

Grandmère, hands clenched, stares out the window. "Sometimes, the best bravery is surviving."

The firefly dances, blinking yellow in the air above the porch. Seeing her, I feel better.

Grandmère cups my face. Her hands are rough, her touch gentle-soft. She kisses the tip of my nose.

I feel better. But I worry whether Grandmère thinks my "who" is stupid. I should've answered "what."

Bear

I wake, humming. Yesterday, I talked silly. *A hero.*
Maybe Grandmère forgot what I said? I know I'm not
special. "Just plain Maddy," as my sisters would say.

I hum quick, bright notes.

Grandmère hums back. Our ritual has begun.

I dress and run to the backyard, thanking Sweet
Pea for her eggs. She clucks back.

Grandmère stirs dewberry syrup. I scramble eggs,
cracking the shells on the side of the pan. Quiet, I set
the table. Grandmère flips griddle cakes.

We eat. Sunlight streams while I gulp water. It's going to be a regular day.

I take another gulp of water. Water is sweeter in the bayou.

I scrape the plates and wash the dishes. Grand-mère dries. Her head bobs like she's still humming our happy tune. I exhale, relieved; maybe I didn't ruin anything.

Grandmère's head lifts; her whole body stills. "Bear's here."

I don't hear anything. I'm scared of bears.

There's a whistle. At least I think it's a whistle.

"*Oui*. Bear's here. Time to play."

"A bear?"

"No, Bear. Come. See." Grandmère opens the screen door. Damp heat smacks me.

"See." She points. A boy, shaggy-haired, sits high in a cypress tree. "Bear."

"It's a boy."

"True, *c'est vrai*. He's your new best friend."

"But I don't know him." I clutch the porch rail.

"You will. Go on. Go play. Quick. *Vite*." Grand-mère shoos me down the steps.

Dragging my feet, I grumble, "What if I don't like him?"

"You will."

I'm reluctant to go. We haven't finished our ritual. "Do I have to?"

"*Oui*. Children should play."

"When should I come home?"

"When you get tired."

"What if it's dark?"

"Don't matter. Stay away all night. Somebody will give you shelter."

I'm exasperated. "What about a cell phone?"

"Don't work here. 'Sides, what for? You'll hear me holler if I need you."

I want to holler, *What if I need you?* I'm nervous. I didn't know I was supposed to make friends.

Hands on her hips, Grandmère smiles, encouraging. Like a squirrel, the boy scrambles down the tree.

"Ma wouldn't be happy," I shout, feeling stubborn.

"Sure she would. You're safe here, Maddy. Enjoy the wild. Bear will keep you out of trouble."

"Won't promise," says Bear with a grin. Fingertips to his head, he tips an imaginary hat at Grandmère.

He's taller than me, big-boned but skinny-legged. His cheeks are red, his brows bushy, thick. His smile is goofy and crooked.

I'm not so sure about Bear. I murmur, "You don't have to play with me."

Bear frowns, his brows meet in the middle. He looks sad.

How can I say I'm feeling shy, fearful, worried, all at once? I look past the bushes and trees. Who knows what's deep in the bayou? What wild things wait?

Why can't I stay on the porch, studying the yard with Grandmère?

Grandmère looks like Ma when she's disappointed in me—lips tight, eyelids lowered, back taut. Even her arms are crossed like Ma's.

Bear kicks the dirt. "I get it," he says, muttering. "Your sisters didn't want to play with me, either."

"My sisters?"

"They never liked running. Never wanted to have any fun."

"You met Layla? Dionne?"

"Aisha, Aleta, too. A different sister each summer," Bear grumbles.

"What?"

"They squealed, scolded me," Bear blurts. "They didn't like dirt, didn't like water. Wouldn't fish. Touch a worm. Or climb a tree."

I can see it—my sisters staring down their noses at Bear and his bayou.

"They didn't like me."

I step back, hearing his hurt.

I look at Grandmère.

Who do you see? Like Sweet Pea, she's talking to me even though she isn't. She stands still, watching me.

Bear's head hangs like it's going to fall off, loneliness weighing him down. This I can understand. Even in a house full of sisters, I'm lonely, sometimes.

Bear tips his pretend hat again. " 'Bye, Maddy."

"Wait!" I swallow, not liking what I'm thinking. "You're sorry you met me."

"Hoped you'd be different," he says, woeful. "Guess city girls just don't like me." He starts walking, fast, bouncing off his toes. Any second, I think, he's going to take off running.

"But I like you!" I shout. "I'm sorry I acted mean." Just like my sisters.

Bear turns. His grin is the biggest I've ever seen.

"Ready for an adventure?" he asks, mischievous.

Am I?

I look past Bear. The bayou seems alive, moving with the breeze.

What did Grandmère say? Said the bayou had been waiting, dreaming forever. I shiver.

From the porch, the bayou is beautiful. But now Bear is asking me to dive into it. Grandmère's urging me, too.

I've never seen so much soft dirt, so many jagged rocks and pebbles. Giant trees, bushes, and weeds, twist and tangle, hiding animals. *Secrets.* Why did I think that?

"Scared?"

Even though I am, I answer, "No."

"Maddy," says Grandmère, startling me, "you're like me. Like my mother and her mother before." She squeezes me, her white hair tickling my cheek. "Brave, isn't that you?" she asks, letting go.

"Come on." Bear whoops, stretching out his hand. It's dirty, strong, calloused. Not soft like city hands. "Catch it."

Something inside me snaps, breaks. I'm ready for something big.

"On land, Maddy," Grandmère mutters. "Bear's your best friend on land."

Grandmère makes no sense.

"I can do water, too," says Bear. "Anyplace you want."

I laugh. Bayou folks are funny strange.

"Come on."

I clasp Bear's hand, hard. He runs, tugging me, leaping over rocks. My arm feels like it'll tear from its socket.

"Faster," Bear shouts. "Faster."

I inhale and burst into my fastest run. Sun pouring down, we're running side by side.

Squishy soil shifts beneath our feet. Sweat runs down my face. A chipmunk darts up a tree. I feel good. Running, I feel free.

Bear yells, "Ya-hoooooo. Ya-hoooooo!"

At home, I never run.

Swamp Tour

"Been on an airboat?" Bending, hands on his knees, Bear breathes deep, gulping breaths.

I'm panting so much my sides hurt. Bear doesn't even wait for me to answer. He's off running again.

I follow, not minding the rasp in my lungs. I feel bold, happy. We come to a clearing. I stop, awestruck.

All around me is green—light, dark, yellow-green, purplish green, turtle and forest green. Plants are everywhere, low weeds and moss carpeting the ground. Up high, tree branches arch, blocking out the sun. It's still hot, but shade makes the air cooler.

Bear watches me. Both of us are still. It feels like we're the only people in the world. Like there is no world, except here.

Head tilted back, legs planted wide, Bear stretches his arms high into the air.

"Why're you named Bear?"

"Not my real name."

"What's your real name?"

Bear grimaces. "Not saying. It's awful."

"Come on, tell."

"Won't. I'm Bear. 'Cause if anybody feeds me, I come back for more." Bear grins. "You don't have any food, do you?"

I shake my head.

"That's all right. We'll catch some. This is the best place. My hideaway." Excited, Bear swings his arms. He walks around the clearing's rim, touching plants. "This here's a Christmas fern. Green, all the time. This here's a royal fern. It's a baby now. It'll grow five feet, big as me." He pauses, his fingers stroking leaves. "Want to see something special?"

I nod.

"Come on. Crawl through."

"What?"

"Come on!"

I get down on my knees like Bear and crawl. I'm glad I have overalls. Moist dirt sticks to my hands, my covered knees. Crawling over swampland, I can see the plants up close. Roots, spiraling deep. Tendrils, shooting up.

My sisters would call me crazy. But just like it felt good running, it feels good getting dirty. Slithering over spongy land.

Bear points. Puts a finger to his lips. Points again.

Belly flat, using my elbows, I inch forward. Deep in a crevice, next to a willow tree, is a small, rough tunnel. "Swamp rabbit hole," says Bear.

"Cottontails. Few weeks old. You have to look close."

I scoot closer, seeing dark, puffy shadows.

"Lay your head down."

Grass tickles my face. I peer, closing my left eye and squinting with my right. I can see a mound of furry gray. Tufts of white, here, there. A small rabbit ear. And another! A black-toed paw nudging another rabbit's head.

Bear inches back. I turn, digging with my elbows, and stand with him.

"They're sleeping," he says, glancing back. "They only come out at night. I've watched them."

Bear sighs with joy. His profile is sharp, angular, straight-nosed. I've never known a boy like him. Chattering then quiet. Chatter. Quiet. Chatter.

Bear rubs his dirty hands on his overalls, so I do, too. And he's off again. "Come on, Maddy. Come on!"

I like how Bear says my name—not "Maddy" but "Mah-dee," making it twang, linger.

"Come on. We're almost at the water." I follow.

Salt fills the air. I wriggle my nose. I smell muck, too; it's getting stronger, but it doesn't smell bad. Smells alive, not like city stale.

"Look." Bear halts suddenly, pointing up.

Aahhhh. A red-tailed hawk glides, arcs across the blue sky.

"Come on."

The landscape changes again. With each step, the forest darkens, thickens. More and more grasses. Endless towering trees. Fallen branches, cracked logs.

Bear swats away willow branches, drooping with shimmering green. "Careful. Water everywhere," says Bear.

Fallen seeds, leaves decomposing, the marsh has become muddier, squishier, blackening my tennis shoes.

We come to a wide stream. The shoreline is chocolate-black with green slime; the water, sluggish, has tangles of algae, duckweed, patches of floating moss. Bayous are stagnant or slow-moving streams, I remember from science class. "Part of our disappearing wetlands," said Miss Avril. "Erosion causes hurricanes to hit New Orleans harder."

"The bayou's got snakes, crawfish. Catfish. Bugs and gators."

"Oh," I exhale, surprising myself, thinking Bear's twang makes even snakes and gators sound good.

We walk a slippery edge between water and marsh grass. If I bend too far left, I'll fall into dark water topped with water lilies and moss. Stalks of wild grass clump, struggling to hold soil together. To keep the boundary between land and water.

"To ride an airboat, Maddy, first, you've got to understand the waterways."

"Like reading a map of the road?"

"That's right. Need to understand where swamp water ends. Where it's safe and unsafe to go."

The stream widens, branching into inlets, like fingers poking deep into land. Currents quicken. Dragonflies flit, land, and flit again.

"Stay close," Bear says.

Then, like exiting a cave, the landscape changes again, brightening, becoming an endless expanse of water.

"The Gulf of Mexico."

"I've never seen so much water." Waves, blue and dull green, roll to shore, creating white foam, collapsing, lapping and licking the sand.

"You can't ride an airboat here," I say.

"Nope. Waves too powerful."

I watch a pelican fly, skirt above the waves. Its long-nosed beak is yellow, spotted red. Its wings reach, flap, and glide. The pelican dives, plucking a wriggling fish.

Bear sits cross-legged on the sand, surveying everything he sees. Sky, land, waves, sun, and birds.

He's used to being alone, I think. He's forgetful I'm even here.

I frown. I'm a second wheel, a "tagalong," like my sisters always complain. Even when I don't want to go, Ma says, "Dionne, take Maddy." "Layla, take Maddy." To the mall. A neighbor's apartment. Their playdates.

Bear doesn't need me here.

"Why're you doing this?"

"What?"

"Taking me along?"

"Queenie told me to. Said you'd like it."

I shudder. "Who's Queenie?"

"Your grandmère."

Grandmère? "She isn't a queen."

"Is around here. Queenie said you needed to find home."

"I've got a home."

"Nobody said you can't have two. 'Sides, if Queenie hadn't asked, I would've wanted to."

"Why?"

"You're Maddy," he answers, matter-of-factly. "You're exploring with me."

I like what Bear says. I'm not the youngest, the littlest—just me. Not just another one of those Johnson girls.

I plop beside him. Waves race in and out, each different as they form—water churning, sunlight glittering—crashing like diamonds.

"My pa has two homes." Bear points. "See, Maddy. Way, way out there, far, far in the Gulf. On the sun's right side."

I don't see anything besides endless water and pancake clouds, but I don't want to disappoint Bear. "I see."

"It's Pa's oil rig. Black metal and concrete slabs. Stilts sunk deep into the water. Platforms are huge. Gigantic cranes, towers with steel drills plunging, twisting like a corkscrew into the ocean floor. See? Do you see, Maddy? Do you?"

I nod.

"Pa's gone most always. Stuck in the middle of the Gulf during storms, hurricanes.

"But he likes the bayou better. Being with me." His whole body slumps.

"Where's your ma?"

"Not here." Bear looks even sadder. "Ma's a one-home person. But it isn't here. 'Texas, maybe,' Pa says. We're not sure."

"Sorry. Didn't mean to make you sad again."

Bear's eyes are deepest brown. He blinks, jumps. "Sad is as sad does. Come on."

"Is that your favorite phrase? 'Come on'?"

"You don't want to come?" Bear looks disappointed.

"Come on," I crow in the biggest, loudest voice. "Come on."

"Ya-hoooo." Bear's smiling again.

I run from the Gulf, back toward Grandmère's home.

"Almost to the airboat, Maddy," says Bear, running in the lead again. "Over here." I follow him, twisting, turning until we come to a small dock.

Surprised, I stop. "Wow."

It's huge. Sitting three feet high off the water is a boat with two high-backed seats and a fan, a thousand times bigger than a house fan, attached to the back.

"Fastest airboat in Louisiana." Bear scrambles up, extends his hand.

Eager, I pull myself in.

"Here. Put these on." He hands me earmuffs, thick and black, like a pilot's.

Bear presses a button and the fan roars, the boat jumps, and we're off!

We bounce over swamp water, startling fish, birds. Screeching, heart racing, grabbing my seat with both hands, I think this ride is better than a roller coaster in an amusement park.

"Ya-hooo!" yells Bear, turning the wheel, making a sharp curve. Both our bodies lean right; I scream. It's scary-fun to think I might fall off. Fun-scary, having the boat kicking up spray. Fun-scary, blades whirling, roaring so loud even earmuffs can't block all their powerful noise. Fun-scary for me and Bear to be shooting like an explosion across the swamp waters.

Bear cuts the engine. I slip off the earmuffs.

We're north of the Gulf, in deep, deep bayou water. It's dead quiet. Weeping willows' branches hang like rope. Patches of moss float in the thick water.

"See the gator?"

I look, but I don't see it.

"It looks like a log. Charcoal gray."

"I see it." And I do. A big old alligator eye slowly opens.

I hold tight to my seat.

Lightning-quick, the gator lunges, its jaws opening like a lion's. *Snap!* Little feet wriggle out of the side of its mouth. I almost cry, "Poor baby turtle." But I clench my mouth. I don't want Bear to make fun of me.

The nasty gator swallows. I sniff.

Bear moves, capable, sharp. He tosses an anchor and reaches behind the seats, pulling out two long sticks with dangling wire, handing me one. Then he lifts a jar, bugs crawling inside. Cockroaches? June bugs? Water bugs?

"Bugs catch fish," says Bear. Catching his bottom lip with his teeth, he focuses on pricking the bug with the wire's hook.

"Yuck," I say.

"Bugs don't mind. They help us catch redfish. That's the way the world works here."

A bug wriggles between his fingertips.

"I don't think I can."

"Sure you can. It's what we do in the bayou. Fish."

I take the wriggling bug. "Sorry," I say to the bug, pricking the hook through its skin. "Now what?"

"We drop the lines and wait."

And wait. And wait.

But the waiting isn't bad. It's like cooking in the kitchen. Quiet, calming. Deep in our own thoughts.

Me and Bear sit back-to-back. Bear's hook dangles off the left side of the boat; mine dangles off the right.

Tiny, tiny bugs flit up, over, and across the water. Birds, mouths open, gobble them up. Fish leap, swallowing them, too. Poor bugs. I guess Bear's right. Bugs expect to be eaten.

My wire tenses. A fish? I lean over the side, peering, trying to see a fat-belly fish swish by, but the swamp bottom is too muddy.

Still, my wire tugs. One—two—three. "I think I'm catching a fish, Bear!"

"Hush, then. Else you'll scare it."

One tug, two tugs, three. I see nothing. Then, a big tug jerks my arm.

I look over the side. A face. Wide, black eyes. I start to yell. A finger touches, crosses her lips. It's a girl, like me. Her face, black and sparkling, skimming beneath water. Long black hair stretching and tangling with the algae and grass, floating in the brown water.

"A fish!" shouts Bear, distracted, reeling in his line.

I look away, just for a second, and when I turn back, the face is gone. Lost beneath the water.

A cold redfish wriggles across my feet. Bear flips open a locker, lowering the fish inside. "Let's get to shore and eat. I'm starved." He starts the engine.

Am I crazy? Should I tell Bear I saw a girl, breathless, covered with water?

Yes, I decide. Bear is a friend. "Bear, I saw... something."

"Always lots to see." He maneuvers the airboat to shore.

He helps me down. "I've been waiting to see you, actually. Four days I had to wait. Queenie said so." He ties the airboat to a log post stuck deep in the water.

"You waited, just for me?"

"Today's day five. Queenie said I'd be 'your surprise.'"

I smile. Bear's a good surprise.

From his overalls, Bear pulls a pocketknife. He cuts off the fish's head, scratches off its scales, then slices its belly. His fingers rip out the guts. I can't look away. I've never seen things caught, killed, and cooked, up close. Only store chicken cut and packaged for frying.

"Thank you, Fish," says Bear. He moves, quick, gathering twigs, thin branches, leaves. From his pocket, he pulls two smooth rocks. He scratches them together, making a small fire. He sticks a branch into the fish's mouth down to its fin. He holds it over the fire.

A different kind of cooking.

"Maddy, in the wild, carry salt and pepper. Queenie taught me."

"To cook?"

"Sure 'nough." Bear pushes his hand deep inside

his back pocket and pulls out a cloth bag. "Pepper and salt mixed. I added dried onions, rosemary from Queenie's garden. My idea. Never know when you catch a fish." The fish, on a stick, spins above the fire. Bear turns it slowly, evenly, so it doesn't burn. It sizzles, pops, crackles.

We eat with our fingers—smacking lips, biting skin and flesh, licking juice from our fingertips. "This is good, Bear."

Bear cooks with his heart. Like me.

"Bear," I murmur, gathering courage. "Beneath the water, I think I saw a girl."

"Can't be," he answers, dousing the fire. "Nobody swims in the swamps."

"She wasn't swimming. More like floating."

"Must've been mixed-up shadows, underwater twigs."

"I saw her, Bear, I'm sure I did."

"Not possible."

"Bear, she looked straight at me."

Bear looks down, staring at ashes, wriggling his bare toes.

"Bear!" I shudder, feeling as though I'm about to ruin the day. What if I'm wrong? What if I didn't see what I think I saw? "Grandmère—Queenie—says you're going to be my best friend. Friends trust friends." I don't tell Bear that I've never had a best friend. Ever.

Bewildered, Bear shakes his head. "Lived here my whole life. Never heard a thing about swamp—"

"—people. A girl."

Bear puckers his lips. Tugs his hair. Any second, I think, he's going to make fun of me.

He looks at me serious. "I don't know everything. Pa says the bayou always has mysteries. Show me, Maddy."

We shake hands.

"Bear, you're the nicest, strangest boy I know."

∽

For more than an hour, Bear revs and cuts the engine. We search and search as the airboat drifts, floats. Section by section, me on the right, Bear on the left, we stare into the dark, murky water. Thick with algae and moss, the swamp barely moves.

"Let's try over here," says Bear. The boat speeds to the left, rounding a curve. The water is a bit clearer. Four turtles sun on a log. For another hour, we search, moving south.

"Fresh water and salt start mixing here," says Bear. "Land erodes, can't hold back Gulf waters. Pa says that's why land's disappearing.

"'People's fault,' Pa says. 'Oil folks dredging canals. Engineers altering the river's course.'"

"Maddy?" Bear taps me on my back, startling me.

I lift my head, my neck hurting from leaning so far over the boat's side. Me and Bear are dripping sweat. Staring, bug-eyed, at water is hard work.

"Do you think this thing—I mean, the girl you saw—likes only fresh water? Or salt? Or both? Maybe we're too far south?"

"I don't know, Bear." Now it's my turn to feel dejected. Nothing to go on, and Bear still believes me. Maybe I saw something because I wanted to see it; just like Bear pretended to see his pa's rig, miles and miles away?

"Maddy, you sure she wasn't dead? Accidents happen. Swamps are dangerous. Just like Pa's rig. A fall, not paying attention, acting like you know everything..." His voice trails off.

Bear's brows squish. He's worrying about his pa.

"Your pa's fine, Bear."

Bear nods, quick. "I know."

He leans forward to turn the boat's key. Touching his shoulder, I stop him. "Alive, Bear. She was, truly. Not dead. Alive."

His expression quizzical, serious, Bear looks at the setting sun. "Time to go in. Next time, Maddy. Next time." He turns the motor on. Fan roaring, we bounce and bump over water, avoiding logs and gators.

∼

At dusk, the sky glows purple-orange. The airboat fan moves slowly as Bear guides the boat to its home anchor.

On land, a puffy-cheeked, red-haired man is flailing his hands. Shouting something I can't hear.

The boat shudders, stops. Me and Bear remove our earmuffs.

"Bear, I done told you to leave my boat alone."

Bear mutters, "See, Maddy. Never promised not to get in trouble." He steps over my legs, leaps onto dirt, and offers me a hand down.

"How many times I told you? Ten? Twenty? Hundred?" The man shakes a fist.

Turning away from me, fingers crossed behind his back, Bear says, "I'm sorry, Mister Cochon. I'm sorry."

C for *cochon*, I remember. "Pig" in my French alphabet book.

Mister Cochon looks like a pig, but in a good way—pot-bellied, soft-skinned, with wispy red hair on his head and arms.

"I was showing Queenie's granddaughter—"

"Queenie's granddaughter? That her?" Mister Cochon waddles close, his chin jutting forward.

"Which grandbaby, you?"

"The youngest. Madison—Maddy."

"Ah. The last one." The way he says it, *the last one*, makes me quiver.

Mister Cochon pays no more attention to Bear, just me. He circles me. I feel shy. Mud, dirt, and grass stains are all over my overalls, hands, and arms. My face is sweat-dirty. If my sisters were here, they'd make fun of me. They'd say, "Maddy doesn't know how to be pretty."

Mister Cochon grunts, like he's satisfied. "You look like Queenie."

I feel proud. Bear winks.

Mister Cochon turns to Bear. "Forgive you this time for taking my boat. Anything for Queenie's granddaughter. Teach her about the bayou. But next time, Bear, ask. Else I'll tan your hide."

Bear grins and we follow behind Mister Cochon, chubby, low to the ground.

"Smelled fish miles away. You cook good, Bear. But fish ain't enough for a growing girl. Need stew. Andouille sausage. Shrimp. Rice." Mister Cochon's hands flail, punctuating the air with each ingredient.

Bear flails his hands, too, making me giggle.

"Yes, now, fish is not enough. Need to blend, mix it up. Feed our guest right.

"Maddy, Maddy, Maddy. Mighty tiny, tiny mighty," chants Mister Cochon.

"Bear," I whisper, "what's he mean?"

"You," Mister Cochon shouts back, leading the way. "Like Queenie. Tiny mighty."

Me?

Firelight

"Meet Queenie's granddaughter," Mister Cochon calls as we near a small town. The tree limbs shake. An owl hoots. "Meet Madison Lavalier."

"Johnson."

"What?"

"Pa's a Johnson."

"You're a Lavalier here," he says, bellowing. "Come meet Madison Lavalier."

I tug his shirt. "Johnson."

"Lavalier," he shouts. Then, more softly, "Johnson."

Pitch-black, beyond the fire, I can't see anything.

Mister Cochon lives in a shack half the size of Grandmère's. His kitchen is outside. A cast-iron pot sits atop crackling wood and burning red stones. His stew smells better than me and Ma's jambalaya. Spicy, savory, garlicky. Gulf fresh.

"Something told me I should cook my special jambalaya today."

I peek into the pot. The shrimp still have shells; the sausage is cut into quarter-sized rounds. Onions and rice float on top of the red broth. Every stew is different.

"What's it need?" asks Mister Cochon. He hands me a spoon. I taste.

"Hot sauce."

"How hot?" Mister Cochon peers at me as if this is the most important question in the whole wide world.

"Very hot."

Gleeful, he smacks his plump lips. Then he shouts like a kid on a playground, "Everybody, everybody, come out. Won't be disappointed. Come on out. Come meet Queenie's grandchild."

Huge fireflies—no, they're kerosene lamps—sparkle between the trees. I catch my breath. It's unsettling to see flames, even if they're trapped in glass, swaying in a forest.

One by one, folks come. Shadows become bodies separating from trees, edging closer to the campfire. Closer to me, Bear, and Mister Cochon. Folks, all colors, live in the bayou. Some are red-haired, some blond or brunette. A stew. They all feel like kin to me. Like a family I didn't know I had.

"This here's Bolden. Catches shrimp. Makes the best haul in the Gulf."

Bolden's thick-bodied and tall. "Haul isn't as good as it used to be, but I do all right." He grunts, sticks out his hand. It's thick, scarred. His hand could snap mine in two.

Everybody watches me.

I shake Bolden's hand. He barely squeezes mine. His grip is the gentlest I've ever felt.

"I'm Pete. Me and Queenie used to play together. We weren't older than you and Bear."

"Really?" Pete's face is raisin-crinkled. I can't

imagine he was ever a boy. Or Grandmère a girl, for that matter.

"I'm Liza. Used to help Queenie take care of your ma when she was an itty-bitty baby." Eyes blue-cataract-white, she is old-beautiful. Almost as beautiful as Grandmère.

I can't imagine Ma being little, either. "Was she good?"

"Too good. Not enough sauce." Liza hugs me, nearly squashing my ribs. "Have you got sauce?"

I'm confused. Ma says, "Be good, Maddy. All the time. I don't want Johnson girls acting like hooligans." And I try. Oh, how I try.

"What's sauce?"

"Adding flavor. Hot peppers. Cooking a fine stew." Mister Cochon hands me Louisiana Hot Sauce. "Shake, little Queenie. Shake."

I dash sauce into the pot. A dozen folks watch, like I'm making magic. I hear murmurs: "Add more sauce." "Best jambalaya." "Can't believe she's here."

I can't believe it, either. The outdoor fire is

beautiful. Chips of wood sparkle and fly. The air smells of sausage and rice.

"Folks like food," says Mister Cochon. "Spice, extra nice."

"Hot peppers, best," says a man in rumpled plaid and jeans, especially pleased. "I'm André," he says, stepping forward, stirring the stew with a wooden stick.

"A little sauce goes a long way, in cooking and in people." He takes the bottle from my hand and splashes a drop on his finger.

"Tiny mighty," he says, looking at me. "Just the right amount of sauce." He touches the hot-sauce dot to my fingertip. "Glad to have you in Bayou Bon Temps."

"Know what that means, Maddy?" asks Mister Cochon. "Bayou Bon Temps?"

"Good times bayou."

"That's right." Mister Cochon bows. "You've made it even better."

"'Cause she's got sauce," says Bear. "She isn't afraid of adventure."

I blush. "Didn't my sisters visit?"

Mister Cochon pats my shoulder. "Your sisters never visited. Never left Queenie's porch. We all hoped you'd be different."

"Glad you like the bayou, Maddy," says Liza.

"Glad you like our home," echoes Bolden.

Some folks nod; some clap; some just smile. They all make me feel welcome.

"Time to eat!" yells Mister Cochon.

Bear grabs the first plate.

I take the second, but after filling it with stew, I hand it to Liza.

Everyone eats. I marvel Mister Cochon doesn't run out of food. It's like he knew a slew of folks were going to share his pot.

Pete blows a harmonica. Another man with a washboard strapped across his chest starts scraping the ridges, making them sing. Mister Cochon squeezes an accordion, in and out, matching the snappy, staccato rhythm. A woman wearing a bandanna plays a fiddle.

"Party," hollers Bear. "Party." He reaches for Liza, bows, then takes her hand and places his other hand on her back. The music is fast, bouncy, jerky. Zydeco. I've heard it but never danced to it.

I look about—everyone's stomping or twirling.

Me and Bear are the only big kids.

Bolden introduces his little ones. Ben. Charlotte. Douglass. None is older than six. They rumple, reminding me of the baby rabbits.

"My wife, Willie Mae. She goes shrimping, too."

Willie Mae, a black braid swinging at her waist, says, "Boat with us. See bayou glory while you still can."

"Thank you, ma'am," I say, respectful. The Boldens look as old and as nice as my ma and pa.

An elder, snapping the only two fingers on his right hand, asks, "Dance?"

I hesitate.

"Don't worry 'bout my hand. Not contagious. Snapper bit off my pinkie and the next. My middle finger got sliced by fishing wire."

"Did it hurt?"

"You bet. But nothin' better than Gulf fishing. 'Sides, I can still snap."

I snap my fingers, too.

"I'm Old Jake." A gold tooth sparkles.

"Old Jake rescues birds," says Bear. "Fixes them up when they break wings, a beak, or a foot."

"Can I help?"

"You bet." He snaps his fingers again. I snap mine.

Hands together, our arms start swinging. Bouncing, we step, dip, step, dip, side-to-side. He lets go one hand, lifts my other hand, and I just know I'm supposed to spin. Twirl like a top beneath his two-fingered hand.

~

"Look who's here—Queenie's come," chortles Mister Cochon.

"Grandmère!" I shout, skipping forward for a hug.

"You had a good day." Grandmère *knows*. She can tell.

She waves to Mister Cochon. A red turban is wrapped about her head. Gold hoops swing from her ears, like she's going to Mardi Gras.

"Cochon, smelled your good food miles away. Brought corn bread to share."

Everyone surrounds Grandmère. Liza kisses her cheek. Bear hops, cheerful, from foot to foot. Bolden gives Grandmère a big bear hug, lifting her off the ground. Willie Mae curtsies as if Grandmère really were a queen.

Grandmère's almost swallowed, dwarfed by bayou folks. Men form an outer circle, while, inside, women and children hug her or kiss her cheek.

Grandmère's coming is a celebration. Folks are drawn to her like bugs to light. She's happy, beautiful.

Mister Cochon winks at me. "I knew Queenie would come." Gleeful, he rubs his palms.

I suspect he wasn't surprised to meet me at all.

He planned this. Everyone did. Like Grandmère planned on me meeting Bear. Another test?

I scratch my head, feeling blind even though I can see.

"Here, Liza, for your arthritis." Grandmère hands her a small jar. "Cochon, I brought you some mint. 'Specially for you. Brings bees to your hives.

"Willie Mae, here's some nice blue thread to finish Charlotte's blouse." Deep blue, the thread shines like Gulf water.

"This'll be perfect."

Small, useful gifts. A cup of rice, a cotton handkerchief, a fishing hook. Grandmère has something for everyone.

"Baby lettuce. For you, Pete. Soft to chew." (He hasn't any back teeth.)

She hands peppermint sticks to Charlotte, Douglass, and the oldest, Ben.

"I hurt," says a woman, fair and tall. "My shoulder, here."

"Come see me, Jolene. I'll make a poultice," murmurs Grandmère.

"*Elle est reine*," Mister Cochon hollers.

Elle means "she." *Reine* means "queen." Grandmère's a queen.

Bolden, Liza, and Pete repeat, "*Elle est reine*."

Then everyone turns and looks at me. The music stops.

Grandmère tilts her head, hands on her hips, her eyes gleaming.

Uneasy, I stare at my feet. I cross my arms over my stomach.

I stub my toe in the dirt, making a small hole. I don't like everyone looking at me. Except Bear's not. I'm grateful. He's standing beside me studying dirt, too.

Grandmère claps, and music squeals, jumps, and swings alive. Folks dance; I tap my feet; Mister Cochon scoops seconds of jambalaya; and Bolden hugs Ben.

"What about me?" asks Bear, pushing forward. "A gift for me?"

Grandmère pulls a silver tin out her basket. "Open it. Filling for a moon pie."

Everyone "oohs" and "ahs" like the sugary filling is gold or magic dust.

Bear opens the square tin. He dips his finger into the filling, then puts his white-sauced finger into his mouth.

"Taste it, Maddy."

I shake my head.

"Try."

I don't want to do it. I didn't like the moon pies I've had at Mardi Gras. Still, I dip my finger and scoop a bit of white fluff.

Mmm. Vanilla marshmallow with a hint of pepper spice. The best filling I've ever tasted. Using two fingers, I scoop some more. Lick my lips to get every last bit.

"Don't need any crust if you've got filling," crows Bear, scooping more and more. "Filling is the best part."

"What about Maddy?" asks Bear. "Did you bring her something, too? Something special?"

Everyone quiets, stills, looks at Grandmère. Looks at me. I don't like being the center of attention.

"Bear's right. Come here, Maddy." Grandmère holds out her hand. A firefly lights on her palm.

"Queenie's pet!" shouts Mister Cochon.

"I'm giving Miss Firefly to Maddy."

"I want one," coos Charlotte. "Me, too," whines Douglass.

Hand outstretched, Grandmère walks to me.

The firefly crosses her hand to mine. It's—no, *she's* the firefly from the car ride. I know it. Black beady eyes. Tiny feet.

"Call them, Maddy," Grandmère whispers. "Call the fireflies."

I gulp. My sisters don't even come when I call. Fireflies? Lightning bugs? Coming to me?

"Call them, Maddy."

I don't say anything. Just watch Miss Firefly.

Pete starts blowing his harmonica. Folks start dancing again. Only Bear sees Grandmère bending her head, whispering to me. He can't hear her, though. He scratches his head.

Wings flapping, my firefly rises to the height of my eye. She's a creature, but somehow not. Her eyes see me like Grandmère sees me. Maybe she can talk like Sweet Pea talks? Or like Grandmère talks, sometimes, without saying a word?

"Miss Firefly, call your family, friends," I mumble.

"You call them, Maddy," says Grandmère.

I blink. Me?

"Call nice and quiet."

"Fireflies," I say, my voice trembling. I swallow. My mouth's dry.

This is silly, I think, about to cry. Other than helping Ma cook, no one counts on me for anything.

I look across the yard. Bear is dancing with little Charlotte. Feeling me watching him, he stops, waves. I smile.

Miss Firefly glows, encouraging me.

"Fireflies, come." Remembering my manners, I add, "Please. Pretty, pretty." I suck in air, then exhale, "please."

Like a gust of wind, like blowing candles on a

birthday cake, a breeze sweeps through. Fireflies—hundreds of them. Maybe thousands. I gasp. Swaying lights streak through air, the sky.

Everyone is speechless, studying the flying lights in the sky. Only the little ones squeal.

A firefly lights on Bear's nose, making him cross-eyed.

Grandmère's eyes say she's proud of me.

I cup my hands together. Miss Firefly sits inside them like a tiny lamp. She's my good-luck charm.

I laugh as fireflies, streaking like lightning, surround me—head to toe, over, above, and about my body. Yellow light cascades. I feel like a Fourth of July sparkler.

"It's wonderful. Isn't it, Maddy?" Bear asks.

I catch glimpses of wondrous, happy faces. Everyone is curious—some extend their hands so a firefly can light; others sway like they're dancing with the streaking lights. Grandmère just stands, eyes closed, as fireflies rest in her hair, on her shoulders and arms.

Bear and I, shoulder to shoulder, squeeze hands as over, behind, and around us, ribbons of yellow-green light swirl.

I can do magic!

I laugh out loud.

Firefly Tales

"Hush and I'll tell you a tale." Grandmère sits like a queen in the porch rocker, her feet flat, arms resting on wood as night air ruffles her hair.

I sit, cross-legged, pleased with myself. My firefly rests on my knee. I want to pet her but she's too, too tiny.

"Ever since Lavaliers have been in America, they've been calling fireflies. Our family secret, Maddy."

"Did Ma?" I ask, but I think I know the answer.

Grandmère pats my head. "No, Maddy. Sometimes

the gift skips a generation. Skips a child. I've been waiting a long time for you."

"Me?"

"Yes, you. You felt it, too, *non?*"

I did. Do. I'm different from my sisters. Different from Ma.

Nobody in my family has dreams like me. Sometimes when I wake, I feel special, as if I've left a mysterious world, part wondrous, part scary.

"Do you dream, Grandmère?"

She cradles my hands. "Dreams are just another way of knowing the world. I dream sleeping. I dream wide awake."

"Awake?" *Did I daytime dream the girl in the water?* "Grandmère, tell me about me," I plead. "Tell me about you. The other Lavaliers."

"I'll tell you," she says, rocking forward. "Been waiting to tell you since the day you were born."

I lean against the post. It's way past bedtime at home. But it feels good being awake after midnight, like I'm growing older, finally old enough.

Miss Firefly flits about the kerosene lamp. Grandmère's eyes grow dreamy, like she's pulling memories from the dark.

"Did you know that when Africans were first captured, Nature cried?"

I shake my head.

"Trees bowed down, their leaves falling, boughs scraping the ground. Mister Wind blew and blew, trying to whip women, men, and children free from their chains. Birds—even the buzzards that scavenge dead things—joined herons, pelicans, and crows, squawking until the sky shook. Clouds turned gray—sun slipped down into Mistress Earth. Lions roared, even though men had guns to bring them down. Gorillas, wailing, pummeled their chests. Elephants trumpeted horror. Earth trembled, but nothing, no one, could stop the slave trade."

Grandmère leans forward, head on her chest, hands wrapped about her stomach like it aches. She lifts her head, staring at nothing; her voice sounds hollow.

"My great-grandmother Membe belonged to a great river tribe. Taught to praise, to believe in Water's wonders, how its sound soothed hearts and spirits. How it cleansed wounds. Provided food for both people and animals. How it nourished and grew life.

"Now, here she was on a ship. Damp, dark, and foul. Folks screaming, crying. Hundreds packed and chained in a tight space like sardines in a can. She was ten, and of all the village girls, she loved the water most. Every day she swam, fished in beautiful waters, clear, cool.

"A day didn't go by when she didn't praise the water spirit, who governed the water. Who infused it with love."

"Water spirit?"

"*Mami Wata.* 'Mother Water.' Goddess of the waters. A mermaid, some may say."

"Like the Little Mermaid? Like *my* mermaid?"

"I don't know this Little Mermaid, only Wata. But there're mermaids in all the world's waters.

"Some say: 'Mami Wata? Nothing but superstition.' 'No such thing as mermaids.' 'A folktale for ignorant people.'

"Others say, 'Sailors see manatees. Otters. Sea cows living in Africa, West Indies, the Amazon. No such thing as water spirits, mermaids.' Others believe mermaids lure ships to rocky shores.

"Since the beginning of mankind, people from the top of the world to its bottom have sworn magical creatures reside in oceans, rivers, and streams.

"Membe's tribe whispered of mermaids who protect and cherish. Both water- and earth-bound life. They honored Mami Wata as the spirit who brought their village joy. Who taught them respect for Nature.

"But, for Membe, joy became despair." Grandmère closes her eyes, pressing her fingertips to her lids.

I stroke her arm.

"Each day more women, men, and children were stuffed inside the ship's hold. Some came from her village; some from afar. Some spoke languages she'd never heard. Terrified, everyone suffered. Cramped, strained muscles, hunger, suffocating heat. The littlest children cried themselves to sleep, then cried some more. The sadness and ugliness broke Membe's heart.

"And then, one day, a voice called, 'Lift anchor.' Membe heard chains rattling, sails snapping, and she knew the boat was taking her away from all she loved.

"Membe cried, 'Wata, save me!' She wanted the currents to stop moving, for waves to die, for water to turn to dirt.

"But it didn't work. She knew, water like blood flows . . . nothing could stop her unwanted journey.

"All day, all night, she cried. Weeping away water in her tears. She wouldn't drink the water given with stale bread. Water had failed her."

"Without water, she'd die."

"*C'est vrai*, Maddy. But Membe hated water, hated it more than the men who'd chained her. 'Water betrays,' she chanted. 'Water spirits fail. Wata never loved me, never loved us at all.'"

"She'd given up hope."

"True, but the second night, and no one knows from where or how, a firefly appeared in the ship's hold."

"Like my firefly?"

"That's right, Maddy. The fly hovered close and gave Membe hope. By day, it disappeared. Come night, it was always there. Blinking, near her head, staying close so she could see it, tiny wings flapping.

"Sometimes Membe pretended to sleep, but when she opened her eyes, the firefly was still there. The firefly calmed her, helped her save her strength. Daylight, chained at the neck, arms, and legs, packed tight on wood slats, the memory sustained her. Behind her eyelids, she kept seeing its flickering light."

Grandmère leans back. The rocker creaks, cracks against the wood. Grandmère inhales, exhales. Breathes like she's risen from water.

A firefly, light as silk, perches on my shoulder.

I don't move.

"Is this"—I open my palm, and the firefly lights upon it—"the firefly that came to Membe?" Her wings twitch like eyelash kisses.

"No, child. That firefly is long dead. But this here is a descendant of the first one. Just like you are descendant of Membe, your great-great-great-grandmother. This firefly has been waiting for you."

"Like you and the bayou?"

Grandmère nods.

"Does she have a name? Besides Miss Firefly?"

My firefly walks from my wrist to my elbow.

"You can name her. Take your time. Fireflies are a special gift. A sign.

"All things in this world can't be seen, Maddy-girl. You've got to learn to read the signs. Signs earth-bound, water-bound, too. All of nature.

"Most folks don't pay attention. Don't really see, smell, touch, and hear, not really. Don't honor how they feel, how feelings can be another way of understanding. If you're lucky, when you need them most, feelings, dreams become intuition, *sight*."

"You mean like *seeing* things? Things that aren't there?"

"I mean like *knowing* things. Past, present, future."

Knowing the past and present is hard enough, I think. I'm not sure I want to know the future. Seems spooky.

Though Grandmère's a little spooky, too. But she's also loving and kind.

"Why do folks call you Queenie?" I ask.

"Sign of respect. Honoring what I know, sense, and feel. Like knowing when rain is coming. What herbs are best for poultices. When a baby's due."

"There's lots to learn," I say. "Like in school?"

"Of a different kind. Membe worked hard on the Lavalier Plantation. That's how our family came to be named.

"Like the firefly, Membe gave hope to others. Helping, nurturing, healing. I've carried the line. Now it's your turn, Maddy."

I puff myself up.

"I believe Mami Wata sent the firefly," says Grandmère. "Membe didn't know...or maybe she was too bitter to believe it was so?

"But both my dreams and my mother, long dead

now, told me that Mami Wata left Africa and swam alongside the ship carrying the kidnapped Membe. As best she could, she tried to provide hope, support, and love.

"For all time, Mami Wata exists, helping whenever she's needed. My mother saw her when she was just about your age, Maddy. Four times, she saw her."

My head spins. African magic lives in the bayou. Do I have it in me, too?

"Have you ever seen her? Mami Wata?"

Grandmère shakes her head. "Being able to see Wata sometimes skips generations."

I think about telling her I saw a face in the water. But what if I'm wrong? What if I make her feel bad because she never saw Wata?

"What else do I have to learn?"

Somber, her voice deep, Grandmère says, "Wear clean underwear."

I'm disappointed.

Clean underwear? I always wear clean underwear. How can that be special? I wrinkle my nose.

"Think, Maddy. Master expected Membe to break," Grandmère says, forceful, loud. "To bow down. Lose her self-esteem. But she didn't. That was her real strength."

"Keeping herself clean?"

"That's right, Maddy-child."

I think hard. "Didn't she ever get dirty?"

"'Course she did. Working in the fields, sunrise to sundown. How could she not? But, chin high, she worked. It's a saying: 'Wear clean underwear.' It means 'have self-respect.' No matter how hard he tried. Beatings. Bullying. Calling her names. Master couldn't take away her self-respect."

"Lesson one: Respect yourself."

With Grandmère, everything's a story.

"Time for bed," she says sternly.

"Did I upset you?"

"*Non*," Grandmère sighs. "I've been telling you what's needed. What's wanted. But you're not ready."

"Ready for what?"

"What's needed."

The porch door slams.

I feel hurt. Then I remember the porch door always slams. It doesn't have springs.

Part of me wants to go home, back to what I'm used to.

But part of me remembers how glorious it felt to call fireflies. It was real. I didn't dream it, I'm certain. But if I did dream a mermaid, is she any less real? Is Grandmère's tale true?

My head hurts. I don't understand what I'm thinking. I try to puzzle it out. There's my known world—New Orleans. A life with my family. My sisters bickering. A world tamed by glass, metal, and concrete.

Then there's an unknown world—Bayou Bon Temps, where Grandmère tells tales, loving and strange.

The night sky darkens. My firefly poses on the porch rail, then another firefly lands, then another, until there are ten tiny fireflies in a row sparkling bright, then brighter. Each one, glimmering, pulses in time with their tiny breaths and hearts.

Fireflies mean hope. Maybe they're telling me I won't disappoint?

Bear likes me. Grandmère likes me, too, I can tell. And though she hasn't said it, she loves me, too.

I inch closer to the fireflies. They're truly beautiful, glowing like mini Christmas lights, making me believe all is going to be fine. It's the middle of the night, but I feel like I'm waking up, understanding more.

" 'Wear clean underwear,' " I whisper. Leaves ripple. A raccoon dashes through the underbrush.

I stoop before the fireflies. "I can do that. Wear clean underwear." They glow brighter, answering back. I feel happier, hopeful.

Bon Temps is a fine place. It's more alive than anyplace I know.

"You're not ready," Grandmère said. I'm not sure what I'm getting ready for. But if Grandmère wants me ready, I can get ready. Like Membe got ready for her hard, new days.

Sayings and Signs

Each day, Bear and I explore.

I tell him Membe's tale, just like Grandmère told me. I'm not certain Bear believes it. But he likes hunting, solving mysteries. If he were a hero in a story, he'd hunt for a pot of gold; search for a dragon's lair; track a golden fleece.

Mister Cochon, though he fusses, lets us borrow the airboat. Each day, Bear races the motor and we fly, bouncing over water. Then we slow, peer at muddy water, algae blooms, searching for the smallest sign.

Dinnertime, we eat stew, boiled shrimp, okra, and corn bread. Whatever Grandmère cooks. Bear eats like there's a hole in his stomach that can't be filled.

Nights, we sleep on Grandmère's porch. "It isn't real camping," complains Bear. I don't care. I've never slept outside before. I've got a pillow, sheets, and the night air is so moist, I'm breathing water.

I see millions of stars. Flickering, glowing. Stars streak across the sky.

The moon watches me. No matter how I shift, turn, the moon holds still, right where I can see it. Each passing night, it grows big, bigger, transforming from a sliver to a crescent moon.

Before sleep, the last thing I see is my firefly darting under and over the porch rail and Bear's brown, shaggy hair.

Only problem is, Bear snores.

~

Mornings, Grandmère wakes us, singing. Not humming, but singing with words. Our ritual has changed since Bear's our guest. There's not as much quiet time for me and Grandmère. I like Bear visiting, but I miss the quiet.

But I think playing with Bear is part of Grandmère's lessons, too. It's like I've finished one set of teachings and now I'm learning set two. I still don't know what I'm studying for, but it doesn't matter. I like being a Bon Temps girl.

Most days, Grandmère's tunes are happy. She sings about slow-moving waters, spirits in trees, and spiders spinning webs with love. Her voice is high, soprano, warbling at times, like a nightingale.

Today her song is sad. I don't understand the French; I only know her mournful sounds make me cry.

I don't ask Grandmère why she's sad. Or what the song means. As far as I can tell, nothing's wrong. Each bayou day seems better than the last. Maybe Grandmère's singing for the past? Or the future?

My sisters are right. Grandmère is a little weird.

I want to be just like her. Just not when she's singing sad.

"Finish breakfast," says Grandmère. Then, "*Vite*, quick. Clean the dishes."

I wash. Bear dries. Afterward, Grandmère orders, "Go play."

But before we're down the steps, she tells us to wait. On the porch, she stands regal, strong. "A saying."

I love this part. Especially on her good singing days.

One day, Grandmère said, "Do good and it'll fly right back to you."

Another day, she said, "Ten isn't just one more than nine. Ten means change. Energy, luck. New things in life."

Mostly, I don't understand a word Grandmère says. But I try.

But on days when her singing is sad, she gives warnings. "If a bird snatches your hair for its nest, your hair will fall right out."

"Ladybug, ladybug, fly away home. Your house is on fire and your children are gone."

I tremble, waiting for Grandmère's saying. She starts singing again. It's a different song but still mournful.

Dodo titit
Si ou pa dodo,
krab la va manje ou
Dodo titit,
krab lan kalalou

I remember this one. Ma sang it. Something like: "Sleep, little one. A crab will eat you if you don't." A bogeyman lullaby. Why do grown-ups like to scare kids to sleep?

Bear and I squirm. We both want to be gone. I don't like when Grandmère's like this. But we wait for the saying.

Grandmère's song fades, petering out like she's lost air. She stares—at what? I can't tell. Instead of her intense gaze, she looks dulled, shaken.

"Why don't you rest, Grandmère?"

She sways, her arms hugging herself. Her head nods, jerks like she's just plucked from the air what she needed to say.

"A bird with a crooked wing means sorrow."

I search the sky for birds. Relieved, I see two hawks soaring, their wings sturdy and strong.

"Another saying," she says.

Two? Before our morning adventure, Grandmère usually just says one. I'm worried.

"Heartache comes in threes."

My shoulders slump.

"Let's go," Bear mutters. "Queenie, we'll help you cook this evening. Maybe fry some fish?"

Grandmère squints, lost in thought, like she's forgotten we're still here.

"Maddy, how old are you?"

Anxious, me and Bear glance at each other. Last few days, Grandmère's asked the same question a dozen times.

"Almost ten."

"Ten's good, Queenie," says Bear, quick, reassuring. "You said, 'Change. Energy. Luck.' If anything bad happens," he boasts, "Maddy will fix it."

He grins, poking fun. "Now, me? I don't fix nothin'. I'm trouble. I'm eleven. You said, 'Patient. Sensitive.' Doesn't seem right. Not me."

I study Bear, his hair tousled, standing on end. He's always tugging, pulling, yelling at me to come on. Yet I think Grandmère's right. Bear is sensitive. Patient when he needs to be. He's a good friend. Kinder than me.

"You're a good boy, Bear." Grandmère stands taller, palms pressed together. "Maddy, I'm beginning to believe you're like me. Did I tell you that, Maddy?"

I nod. I'm a Lavalier like Grandmère's a Lavalier. We look for signs. We call fireflies.

I'm just trying to get ready. For whatever it is. Whatever is coming.

Grandmère starts singing again. Her voice scratches and wails. Bear crouches, covering his ears.

I holler, "Stop, Grandmère. Please. Too sad."

"Lesson one." She points one finger. "Self-respect. Two." She points another. "Signs everywhere, Maddy. Pay attention." Then she motions me close. "Play." Her voice is desperate. "Enjoy the bayou while you can."

"Make me a birthday cake?" I ask, trying to distract her.

"Moon pies," she answers. I see myself inside her eyes. A small shadow. "Moonlight reveals mysteries."

Nervous, I bite my lip.

"Extra filling, please?" begs Bear.

I jump off the porch. "Come on, Bear." I look at him, pleading, *Let's explore.*

Bear understands what I don't say. He clutches my hand. We run.

Grandmère's sad, sad song chases at our heels.

Another lesson. *Pay attention. Signs everywhere.* I open my eyes wide, wider, widest, trying to see.

Fish Tails

"Some in the world don't believe mermaids are real. But some do," I say, perched on the airboat.

Water slaps against the boat's bottom.

"Even though she's never seen her, Grandmère believes Mami Wata is real. But maybe now, she isn't sure? It's been so long since slave days. Maybe she thinks Mami Wata has swum back to Africa? And that's why her songs have turned so sad? Maybe, like Membe, she thinks Mami Wata has abandoned her? Abandoned Bon Temps and all the Lavaliers?"

Bear doesn't answer. He keeps peering into brackish water. His sweaty T-shirt sticks to his back.

It's been over a month. Thirty-two days, we've searched.

When the sun is shining ever so fierce and hot, we search. When rains pour, drenching our skin, we search. When the sky is overcast, gloomy, we search.

I tell Grandmère's tale over and over again, trying to inspire me and encourage Bear.

"Wouldn't everyone in the whole world be happier if mermaids were real?" I clench my hands, nervous.

Bear still doesn't speak.

Worried, I stare at the water and marsh grass. My eyes hurt.

Summer is flying fast.

Without meaning to, I feel like I'm ruining everything. Ruining me and Bear's first and maybe only summer. But I can't give up.

I've read lots of books but never read a tale anything like Grandmère told me. I've seen pictures of brown-, blond-, and red-haired mermaids with white faces. I never thought a mermaid might look like me. I don't tell Bear this, even though I think he'd understand.

I don't tell Bear, either, that Membe is Grand-mère's great-grandmother. I don't tell him she's my kin.

Today, Bear asks, not unkindly, "Maddy, you sure you saw a face? Maybe it was just a fish with bug eyes?"

I don't blame him. I'm ready to give up, too.

"Maybe it's a manatee? Or a lost dolphin? Oh, oh, I know," says Bear. "An undiscovered monster? Something with two heads, big teeth, and a tail that stings, paralyzes.

"Who knows," he says, sounding like Dracula, "what creatures live in the deep?"

Fear rises, grips my chest. I gulp. What if it *is* a monster? We're alone. Searching for our doom.

Whoosh.

I screech. *Splash.*

"Just a gator." Bear laughs. "Still like a log, then quick, pouncing into water. Probably ate a catfish."

I exhale.

Bear zooms ahead, then cuts the engine. We float on the airboat throne. On the left, Bear peers into water; on the right, I look, too. We both focus on the dark, deep water.

"There!" yells Bear.

"Where?" I lean over his shoulder.

"Aw, a diamondback." A snake, dark olive green, with a pattern of diamond shapes, wriggles through the water.

"Poisonous?"

"Naw. Eats toads and slow fish. You're thinking of diamondback rattlers. This one's a plain water snake."

Staring too hard, my eyes hurt. I feel woozy. I fill a tin cup with water from the Coleman cooler. I gulp, fill the cup again and again.

Bear turns the engine key. The fan, behind us,

whirls. Earmuffs on, we're moving fast, the airboat shuddering, rattling, skimming across the water.

I poke Bear. "Eyes." I poke his back. "Eyes!" He shuts the engine.

"What?" he asks, taking off his earmuffs.

"There. Eyes."

"Lilies." He shakes his head. "Just lilies trapped by algae."

"No, eyes, Bear. Definitely eyes," I say, hoping wishing can make it so.

"Lily centers, Maddy. Sometimes brown, yellow specks. Sometimes full-bloom flowers."

Disappointed, I lean back, putting my feet up on the dash.

I'm wasting my time and Bear's. And Bear's been so nice about it, sitting quiet, staring into muddy water, when we could be playing.

"You sure you saw it, Maddy? I believe you, I do. But are you sure?"

"Sure," I say, emphatic, but it hurts to say it. "I'm sure. Just like I'm sure I'm going to turn ten."

Bear squints, nods. He knows when to be quiet.

"Tomorrow," I whisper. "Please, let's try again tomorrow." I don't say "for the thirty-third time." Neither does he, but I bet he's thinking it.

Bear revs the engine. Our earmuffs block the sound. It's quiet. Though he doubts, Bear still helps.

"Thanks, Bear," I say. He can't hear me. I tap his back and smile. Bear smiles back. Not a big smile, but he does smile. I'm grateful.

We head back toward Bon Temps. We both sway as the airboat tilts left, right. Pressure builds inside me, scratching, clawing, plaguing me as we draw closer and closer to land. Another failure.

I feel like a squashed bug. I'm trying hard, trying to learn all Grandmère's been teaching me. But I just *know* that finding, seeing Mami Wata is important. Grandmère's given me so much, and though she hasn't asked, doesn't even speak of it, I hear wistfulness when she tells Membe's tale.

Finding Mami Wata would be my gift for Grandmère.

Bear maneuvers the airboat to its mooring. It's not a full-fledged dock, just a wood post plunged deep. He leaps off the boat, his feet sucking up mud.

"Pa's coming," he says, knotting the line.

"Bear, that's wonderful. Why didn't you tell me before?" I leap off the airboat, slip a little, and catch myself.

"I don't know," says Bear, shrugging. "Pa's been gone over a month. Supposed to be fourteen days on, fourteen off. But he did an extra shift.

"Won't be staying at Queenie's. Staying with Pa."

"'Course, Bear." I wipe my hands on my overalls. "Can't wait to meet him. Maybe he and my pa can be friends."

"Yep. Maybe.

"My pa's the strongest, smartest man in the whole world," Bear says.

I've never heard him this proud.

"The best pa. He's got a beard, Maddy. Did I tell you that?" Bear's speaking fast.

"A beard that rests on his chest. Both soft and

scratchy. He'll take us fishing, Maddy. Pa always catches the biggest catfish. Once he caught Old Lucien—two feet long, fifty pounds. Pa threw Old Lucien back, said such an old catfish deserved to live on. Wasn't that nice, Maddy?"

"Real nice," I say.

Bear's glistening with sweat, his hair flat and wet against his neck.

Pay attention. Something's wrong—I know it. I can *feel* it, hear it in what Bear isn't saying.

Days are getting stranger. Grandmère's sad songs. Odd warnings. Bear rattling, nervous? Just about his pa?

Dark beneath the willows, the day is darkening more. I look up. Drifting clouds fill the space between treetop branches and leaves. I sniff. Rain? Far off, I hear herons shriek. I hear animals scuffling in the bushes. A raccoon? Baby rabbits?

"Let's go," says Bear, not looking at me. "Maybe we should go see if Queenie's all right?"

"Good idea, Bear," I say. But I can tell he's thinking more about his pa than Grandmère.

I turn, scanning the shoreline and water. There're

tons of shadows—some still, some moving. Bayou animals and hot breezes rustling willows. Nothing new.

"Come on, Maddy."

I can't see Bear anymore. He's deep in the forest. Yet I can't move. Swamp water calls. Something— *someone?*—is holding me here.

There's a *swish-swish* behind the airboat. Lapping currents? Old Lucien?

Swish-swish.

I step forward, crouching, trying to see deep. I spot it—a shape, something long as a gator.

Excited, I lean flat, not minding the dirt and dead leaves on my arms and clothes. *Please be real, please be real.*

Something flicks—a tail?—kicking high out of the water. Then disappears.

I blink. Nothing. The water is flat, calm.

Frustrated, I pound my fist. I'm not *seeing*, not even daydreaming. Crazy, my eyes are seeing what I want them to see.

It's been an awful day. Grandmère's fearful. Bear's uneasy. Nothing got discovered.

The bayou feels unsettled. I'm unsettled. Swamp mud can swallow anything. I wish it would swallow me.

"Maaaah-deeee." Sound echoes from far off.

I stand, hollering, "Coming, Bear."

As I turn, I see a flicker. A hand rises from the water and waves. Then, just as quickly, it's gone.

My whole body shakes. *Fingers.* I'm scared. This time I know what I saw. But maybe I'm not ready after all?

Missing Bear, Missing Water

I feel grumpy. Moodier than my sisters when Ma doesn't give them what they want, like TV or extra sweets. Haven't seen Bear in three days. He's with his pa. I'm not jealous; I'm happy for him. But I miss him.

I miss his help searching swamp waters. Miss telling him I'm sure. Surer than before. I haven't had a chance to say *Fish don't have fingers.*

All week I've searched by foot. It's not the same as motoring on an airboat. There are hundreds, thousands of miles of water to explore. I'll never solve the mystery. Maybe's it's crazy to think I ever could?

My only joy left is Grandmère's lessons—her sayings and signs. They lift me up. Except when they're creepy and sad.

New Lessons

Grandmère and I snap pole beans. Quiet, without words, we snap. *Snap, snap, snap.* Our bowls fill with green bits.

I love gardening. Working on the porch. Sweet Pea struts and clucks, pecking at seeds. Her feathers ruffle, but she's just preening.

"Just 'cause you can't see it, doesn't mean it isn't there," Grandmère says out of the blue.

"Is that another lesson?"

"*Oui.* Things seen, unseen."

"Said I saw Bear's pa's rig when I didn't."

"It's there all right. Wish it wasn't." She sighs.

"Why, Grandmère?"

She doesn't answer.

"Smell the wet in the air?"

I sniff.

"Less wet or more?"

I sniff again. Who knew damp air smelled musty green? Like grass soaked with rain.

"Take your time, Maddy."

I inhale deep. Gray. I think I smell it, a sour beyond the green. *Trouble's coming*, I think, without knowing why.

"More, more wet," I say, emphatic.

"Good, Maddy-girl. Storm's coming. Maybe not today or tomorrow, but it's coming. Hovering, breathing over the Gulf, ready to pounce."

"How do you know?"

"Bayou folks follow old ways. City folks forget. Living close to nature, you need to keep yourself extra safe. Can't let blue sky, sun, and bright clouds fool you."

"See our garden?" I tilt my head. "Just 'cause you can't see the roots, doesn't mean they aren't there."

"That's right, Maddy-girl."

"There's life above, below the earth. Above and below water, too."

Grandmère grins, ear to ear. She's pleased. I can tell.

The beans are all snapped.

"Why do you wish Bear's pa wasn't on a rig?"

"'Cause he hates it. You'd hate, too, if work you did spoiled what you love. After slavery, people got better at loving one another. But we didn't get better at loving the land. Miles and miles of land, just gone."

"Gone?"

"Disappeared. Started with merchants, farmers. Folks wanting to move goods quicker up and down the river. I'm old enough to remember when the Army Corps of Engineers started messing with the Mississippi. Building levees to make a straighter ride. Didn't plan on changes affecting the land itself. Changes stopped silt from making new land."

"What's silt?"

"Clay, sand, dirt. Used to deposit at the river's mouth. Made new land. With no silt, land started disappearing. Salt water mixing with fresh didn't help. Fewer oysters, shrimp. Plants started dying."

"What's it got to do with Bear's pa?"

"Oil companies dredged canals in the bayou, laying pipes, made the problem worse. There's been oil spills, too. Sickening the bayou. Killing fish."

"But I thought Bear's pa worked in the middle of the Gulf?"

"Nobody knows what harm is happening in the deep. Oil companies promise 'no harm.' But in Bon Temps, we know better. Deep inside the Gulf water, there might be harm."

"You mean harm we can't see?"

"That's right, Maddy-girl. Just 'cause we can't see it, doesn't mean it isn't real. Isn't there. Wounds, disasters we don't know about, can't see, might already have happened."

Grandmère stands, shaking herself, shaking away sad thoughts. "Let's boil water, Maddy. Cook these beans."

We enter the cottage. Set a match to wood chips. I add salt to the water in the pot.

Salt helps water boil faster. But it destroys land, freshwater life.

The water bubbles, making tiny air pockets. I stare. "Things seen, unseen," I murmur.

Can't see salt. It's invisible.

Next to the stove is a can of lard. I reach for it and scoop spoonful after spoonful of white blobs into the water. They melt.

Grandmère watches, says nothing.

"Oil doesn't disappear like salt."

Quick, into the pot, Grandmère dips a shiny spoon. When it rises, it's dull white, slippery, and wet.

Using pot holders, I pour the hot, slick-filled, greasy water outside. Sweet Pea clacks, tiny wings flapping, and runs away.

I can't cook beans in oily, too-salty water.

Filling a new pot, I try to piece together my thoughts. "Bear's pa works on an oil rig," I say. "But he loves the bayou."

"Loves it, Maddy-girl. Just loves it."

"He's like a grown-up Bear?"

"Used to be. Gotten crusty. He's a good man, but complicated. All twisted inside."

Grandmère pours beans into the simmering water. They bubble and roll like tiny green logs. "Imagine Bear, grown."

I've never imagined a kid being grown. But, in my mind, I can see Bear tall, arms crossed over his chest, his hair even bushier, grinning. Happy.

"Imagine Bear, grown, day in and day out, doing work that might harm his home. But he needs a job. Money. Cars need oil. Someone's got to drill."

Grandmère's voice lilts, her lovely sound making the words more awful.

"Imagine Bear trapped, all day, all night, weeks at a time on a metal-and-concrete rig, sucking thousands of gallons of black, slick, crude oil from the ocean floor. Imagine Bear living on a platform speck in the middle of the Gulf, far from the bayou."

"He'd be lonely," I say. "Lonely all the time."

"That's right, Maddy-girl."

I shiver. Froth sticks like glue to the pot's sides.

I don't want to imagine Bear grown, working on a rig like his pa. He'd be so unhappy. Wouldn't be Bear without the bayou.

~

All day, I think and think on the porch.

Grandmère offers me food, but I turn it down. Sweet Pea pecks dirt at my feet.

Beyond Grandmère's yard, there are herons, rabbits, turtles, gators, and snakes, twisting on land, swimming in water. Plants that droop, shiver, and sway, making shady caves that shimmer with mysterious life.

Bayou folks are the best. I like visiting Bolden, the shrimp boat captain; Willie Mae, his pretty wife; and their kids. Liza grows vegetables and herbs. Old Jake raises chickens and saves hurt birds. Even Bolden's little Douglass knows how to catch fish.

Everybody, young and old, lives off the water and land.

What'll happen if Bon Temps disappears?

Where will folks go?

Grandmère wouldn't be happy in New Orleans.

My head hurts.

Oil is energy. Energy is good. But what if you can't get oil without causing harm? To land, water, animals? People?

Environment. It's a gold-star spelling word.

Saving the environment is harder than fractions. Harder than getting my sisters to be nice. Harder than dreaming nightmares. Or searching for mermaids.

Living My Own Tale

Nights on the porch, I can't sleep. I'm not scared to sleep outside. I love the night sky, the moist air, and cricket and raccoon sounds. My firefly glows.

But nights alone, I imagine Bear grown. An oilman. I feel like I'm suffocating. Like something is pushing hard on my chest. I squirm beneath my sheet, try to breathe slow and deep. I just want to see my friend climbing trees, crawling in the dirt, peeking in rabbit holes.

Grandmère won't let me visit Bear. She says, "Bear and his pa need time."

Time for what? I don't want to lose another day. Don't want summer to end.

Time should STOP so Bear and I can have adventures. Find Mami Wata.

I sigh. Doesn't seem fair it's taken this long for me to have a bayou summer. Taken this long for me to get to know Bear.

As if she knows what I am thinking, Grandmère says, "Don't be selfish, Maddy."

"It's already July. Summer's going too fast."

"Bear and his pa need time."

"T—i—m—e," I whisper into the night air, stretching the word like rubber. "T—i—m—e."

Time for what? Grandmère won't say. I punch my pillow.

My firefly flits and rests beside my head. Wings lazily flapping, her belly pulsing, she's my own private night-light.

My eyes feel heavy. Warm breezes stroke my face. I smell mint, honeysuckle, and damp earth.

"Be green," we learned in school, but I didn't really understand. Here I touch, feel, and smell green. Nature isn't just a picture in a book, or locked behind glass in an aquarium, or caged in patches and pots in a botanical garden.

"I saw a girl in the water," I say to my firefly. "It means something. I know it does. Some lesson 'specially for me."

She glows brighter.

I'll see Bear again, I know. I just hope it's soon.

I fall asleep, dreaming.

There's no sound in the world.

No sound is scarier than a roaring hurricane. No sound feels as empty.

The sky is blue with white clouds. A thin black line, like a black felt marker, marks the horizon, where sky meets water. It's thin but spreading, growing taller, wider, expanding like black inky fingers across the water. The blackness is thicker than water. Slick, sticky. It covers me. I'm drowning. Black crude drags me down.

Wake. Wake. I scream and bitter oil streams down my throat.

I wake, panting.

A ghost. Standing at the porch rail. *White glowing hair and robe.*

I'm still dreaming—no, I'm awake.

Then I see the feet. Tiny, brown feet. Grandmère's feet. She has a bunion on her left big toe.

"Grandmère?"

She doesn't move.

"Grandmère."

Motionless like a ghost, her eyes are drooping and blank.

"Grandmère?" I grip her hand. "Let me take you back to bed."

"Where am I?"

"With me, Grandmère."

Her eyes focus. "Maddy? How'd I get here?"

"Sleepwalking." Layla said Grandmère sleepwalks. I didn't believe her.

Grandmère's fingers are small, her hand fragile. "Come, Grandmère."

"Tiny mighty. Tiny mighty," she murmurs. "I'm getting old, Maddy. Slowing down."

"No, Grandmère," I murmur. I can feel the difference between my hand, Ma's hand, and Grandmère's. Like bayou land disappears, I sense, one day
Grandmère will, too. It isn't fair. I'm just now getting
to know her.

I help Grandmère sit on the edge of her bed. She
touches her nose to mine, kisses my forehead.

"All my life I've been waiting. You were the last
hope. I thought magic deserted our line. Your sisters
saw the world too real. You need space in your mind.
Space for imagination."

"I've got space."

"I know you do. I'm counting on you to hold
together Bon Temps. To keep the stew spicy and
strong."

"Like a good jambalaya?" I sound silly, but I don't
know what else to say.

"The best jambalaya." Sighing, Grandmère lies,
curling her knees to her chest. I kiss her forehead.
Like she's the child.

I tuck the sheet beneath her chin.

Eyes closed, skin soft as silk, Grandmère looks

like an older version of Ma. An older version of me. It's scary but comforting. I feel how deeply we connect. Blood, bones, and skin.

Seeing Grandmère peaceful, eyes shut, not looking at me, I feel brave.

"I've seen something, Grandmère."

"What, Maddy?" she murmurs, eyes closed.

"A girl in the water."

Grandmère opens her eyes. *"C'est vrai?"*

"Twice. A water spirit, a mermaid."

Grandmère sits up, smiling, her face glowing. "How I hoped. How I hoped you'd see her. It's Mami Wata. I know it. I just know it."

"She's real?" I can't help but ask even though I've been searching for weeks.

"My mother saw her. Once I might've seen her. Out of the corner of my eye, I saw a tailfin, but when I turned—nothing. It's been almost seventy years. I didn't think I'd live long enough—" She breaks off into a sob.

"Don't cry, Grandmère."

"These are happy tears. Mami Wata will always

be real as long as someone believes. To *see* her means something else. A different kind of magic."

"Ma, my sisters—none of them saw Mami Wata?"

"When you called the fireflies, I had hope. Hoped your gift would be stronger than mine. Like my mother's."

There's an inkling...a scratching in my mind.

"I need to go, Grandmère. Got to run. Find the mermaid." I pull up my overalls, stuff my nightgown inside.

Grandmère looks lost again.

I pause. "Come with me, Grandmère?"

"*Non*, Maddy." Grandmère shakes her head. "Mami Wata chose you."

I give Grandmère the biggest hug. We both hold tight. "I'm glad I came, Grandmère."

"I'm glad you did, too." Her arms release me. "Now, go. Run. *Vite*. Run, my Maddy-girl."

I run. Bam. Out the front door. Jump over the steps.

I run faster than I've ever run before.

Triumph?

I run. It's dark but I know exactly where to go. My feet don't stumble. They know the path to water by heart.

I pass ferns, pass the rabbits' den. I don't shudder when I hear owls hoot. Or hear snakes swishing in the grass.

I feel like I'm home.

I breathe deep. Exhale. Run. Run. Run. My feet pick up speed. I feel damp air, see night stars, and smell deep green.

Oh, how I wish Bear were here.

Miss Firefly darts, dips, and dives around me as I run. "Come, fireflies," I shout into the quiet air. "Come."

Blinking lights cascade.

Fireflies surround me as I run and run some more.

My feet take me to an inlet where I've never been, just above the airboat dock and the trail to the village.

I halt.

I've seen this place before. In Ma's kitchen. Inside my mind. I saw myself—on this shore, a full moon high, mirrored in blue-black waters.

Like Grandmère, I must've dreamed while wide-awake.

Standing on land's edge, I peer into the water. The surface shines, glitters from starlight and moon-light. I think how water connects and flows from the Mississippi through the swamp, rivers, and streams. All heading south to the Gulf.

"*Blood flows like river water*," Ma says.

For the first time, I understand what she means.

There's all kinds of history inside me. People, living, like Grandmère, Ma, and Pa. People, dead, like Membe and her children and children's children. And all kinds of other people I don't know. I'm mixed-blood. Just like everybody else in the world.

"Every stew is different. Special."

Grandmère couldn't find Mami Wata.

"But I will," I say aloud.

The moon glistens vibrant white. It seems alive. Everything in the bayou seems alive. Even things without a heart: the mud sucking at my feet; the air brushing my skin; and tree limbs reaching out to me.

Fireflies hover above the water's center.

"Come," I call the water spirit. "Please. Pretty, pretty please." The fireflies like my good manners. "Please."

Nothing.

Disappointed, I tremble.

With my whole heart, I say, "I know you exist. Not just in stories."

Nothing happens.

"Please, please come."

Nothing.

I move closer, edging my toes into the water. "I know your name. Come, Mami Wata. My fireflies are waiting."

I see water rippling, spiraling into wider and wider circles.

"Mami Wata?"

Faster and faster, water moves, spraying, foaming into a huge wave.

Up, up...rising from the dark waters I see a girl, beautiful, velvet black. Curls of blue-black hair fall to her waist. She keeps rising above the swamp waters.

I gasp. Below her waist, she's shaped like a fish. Scales shimmer blue, green, silver, and purple. Water drips.

Poised in the air, the moon looks like Mami Wata's crown. Back and tail arching, arms outstretched, palms pressed, her body jackknifes and dives.

"Wait!"

Beneath the water, there's a streak of motion, waves rushing and roaring toward the shore.

I stumble back.

A face appears. Mami Wata doesn't look any older than me. Head tilting, her wide eyes gaze at me. Her lashes are thick, her nose pointy and small. She's smiling.

She reaches out her hand. I clasp it, shivering at the damp cold.

Mami Wata tugs me and I fall. Water closes over my head, filling my nose and throat. I panic, choke. I kick hard but Mami Wata's arms chain me.

I twist, jerk. Muddy water blinds me. I'm going to die. I'm never going to see Ma, Pa, or my sisters again. Never see Bear or Grandmère. I made a mistake. I shouldn't have come here alone.

My lungs ache; my ribs are nearly cracking. Mami Wata's tail drives us deeper and deeper below water.

Slippery tendrils—plants? an eel? fish tails? snakes?—brush against my face and clothes.

I feel light-headed, a quieting darkness like sleep. This is what it feels like to drown.

But then...

Lips touch mine and I feel...bubbles, air. My eyes open. From the inside, Mami Wata glows like a hurricane lamp. I can see her beating heart.

Moving close again, she blows a trail of tiny white bubbles from her mouth to mine. Instead of choking, I breathe.

I breathe water as easy as air.

Mami Wata no longer grips me. Holding my hand gently, she snaps her tail. Whoosh. We glide.

She points to her tail, then to my legs. I flutter-kick. We move, quickly, against the current, our palms cupping water. Redfish and speckled trout dart.

Mami Wata laughs. At least, I think so. I hear a high tremor like harp strings.

She stops swimming, pulling me upright. Her powerful tail slaps. Up, up, we fly, rushing like a rocket to the surface.

The sky is a blue-black comforter. The moon is white, like the creamy filling in a moon pie.

Side by side, we float. Warm water beneath us, warm air stroking us.

Against the dark sky, hundreds of fireflies gleam-blink.

We travel onward. I splash a lot but my mermaid moves smoothly, like the water parts before she reaches it.

I stick out my tongue and taste salt.

We've traveled downstream to the Gulf of Mexico. Just like Bear and I did in the airboat. Wata and I have swum so far.

The Gulf seems endless. Water flows, stretches back to Africa.

Wata, my name. Wata, I think I hear. *Mother Water.*

Treading water, I look closely at the dark face. It's comforting that Wata looks as young as me. But I *feel* an otherworldliness, how ancient she is.

"Maddy," I say. "My name is Maddy."

Wata smiles like she already knew.

Hard Lessons

I wake, lying on the inlet bank, smelling like decomposing leaves. I sit up. The sun is straining, peeking through bushes, around trees.

Where is she? Mami Wata?

The water is smooth, empty. My clothes and hair are dry. It was a dream? It seemed so real. I thought I had done it. Found Mami Wata. But I didn't.

I feel sorry for myself. Pity. Dawn, Miss Firefly and her kin are gone. I feel abandoned.

I remember Grandmère's lessons. *Self-respect. Pay attention. Leave space for imagination.*

I exhale.

An owl hoots. A breeze flutters through the bushes and trees.

On the far shore, I see Bear's rabbits, nibbling on leaves. I hope the owl doesn't pounce.

I try to puzzle it out. Awake or dreaming, stories mean something. They're a kind of truth.

Isn't that what Grandmère's been teaching?

Mami Wata is alive, even if she lives in my imagination. My mind.

I swam with a mermaid!

On my belly, I scoot and wriggle toward the water's edge. "Mami Wata," I call. "Mami Wata." My spirits lift. "Just 'cause I don't see you, doesn't mean you're not there."

The water doesn't answer. Mami Wata doesn't appear.

No Time to Tell

"Grandmère!" I holler, running fast over moist land, kicking through grass and brush. The sun warms my back. Nearer to the house, I smell sweets simmering. Cinnamon. Brown sugar. Vanilla. Moon pies.

Sweet Pea clacks. Her tiny wings flutter. I leap the porch steps, two at a time.

"Grandmère, I saw...saw Mami Wata. She's been here all the time."

"Thought so. Eat," she says.

I'm starving. I chew, swallow, talk. Chew, swallow, talk.

"Water holds all kinds of fish. Single fish, schools of fish, moving, always moving. Bugs cloak about the surface." I bite bacon. "Gators are huge, like rock, seen close. They didn't chomp me, though." Scrambled eggs melt in my mouth.

"Every animal knew the mermaid. She is a Queenie in the water like you're Queenie on land."

Grandmère smiles like it's Christmas. "Tell me more."

"I breathed water. I was a mermaid, too."

Grandmère cradles my cheeks. "Of course you were." She kisses me on the forehead, the tip of my nose.

"Can I tell Bear? I need to see him."

"There'll be time enough. Eat." She slips another slice of bacon on my plate.

"I could take him moon pies."

"They're not ready." Grandmère's face crinkles like walnut skin.

My eyes feel heavy. I feel like my body is being weighted, pulled down to the ground.

"Sleep, Maddy-girl." Grandmère guides me to my cot.

"It's morning," I murmur.

"A nap, then. You've been out all night."

"I should tell Bear."

"There's time. Sleep, Maddy." She tucks me in bed. "You've had a wondrous time. Rest."

I feel overwhelmed. I've seen and felt so much. Stories—real and imagined—are powerful.

I clutch Grandmère's hand. "You won't go anywhere?"

"I'll be right here," she says, stroking my hair. Something about Grandmère's tone isn't right. It's not quite carefree. I don't understand, but I'm tired now. There'll be time to think.

"You're getting ready. Almost there," I hear before falling deeper into sleep.

"Almost ready," I murmur, falling asleep, feeling the happiest I've ever felt.

Spiderwebs shift into patterns like a kaleidoscope. Out of the walls, spiders troop. A dozen. Two dozen. A hundred.

Liquid secretes from their tiny mouths. It's not silk—it's oil soaking webs, transforming them into wet black lace.

Drip-drip.

Black specks stain my sheet. Oil falls on my cheeks, brow, and lips. Oil tastes bitter.

Drip-drip.

Oil stings my eyes, drains into my ears, nose, and throat.

I gasp, open my eyes. The ceiling's webs are grayish white. I don't see any spiders and the window is letting in moonlight, not sunlight. How long did I sleep? Dream? I've slept all day and into the night.

I slide back the curtain. Without turning from the stove, Grandmère says, "Glad you're up. There's a plate of ham and greens."

The table is set for dinner. I'm not hungry, just thirsty. My dream has shaken me—it's a truth, too. Past? Future?

From the pitcher, I pour water. I wash my hands extra with the soap. *More strength, more courage,* I think.

"You want to go, Maddy?"

"Yes, please. I'm not hungry."

Grandmère laughs. "If I was younger, I'd want to

swim with a mermaid, too. Here." She holds out the basket. "In the bottom is your swimsuit. A towel. In case you get wet this time."

I smile. Grandmère's teasing. "Take off your shoes, too."

I hug her, feeling her heart beat, hearing her blood flow. "Thanks, Grandmère. You're not worried about me?"

"No, you'll be fine. Just worried about the bayou." She kisses my cheek. "I want it to be here when you're as old as me."

I kiss her once, twice, then again. "I love you, Grandmère."

"I love you, Maddy-girl." She squeezes me again. "Go now. Have fun."

I open the screen door, jump the steps, and I'm off. I look back at the cottage. On the porch, I can't help but think Grandmère looks like a ghost again.

Not tiny mighty—just a small, old woman with white hair quivering in the breeze.

I bite the corner of my lip and it bleeds. I keep running. No time to tell Grandmère about my spider dream.

Mami Wata

Sitting, watching water twist, surrounding rocks, fallen logs, and grass, I think Louisiana is all water. Wetlands everywhere. A perfect home for mermaids. Do they prefer fresh or salt water?

"Wata," I call. "Mami Wata."

Do mermaids have chores? Work? Do they spend their days hiding from people? Or do they just play? Explore? Watch over those who believe in them and those who don't?

Behind a bush, I take off my shoes and slip on my bathing suit like Grandmère said.

*   *   *

"Wata?"

Bugs flit above water, a fish jumps, and a turtle and its two babies flap little green-speckled legs. Across the shore, I see frogs and gators. A heron glides over water and rests on a branch.

The moon shines bright. "Wata."

The water is sluggish as ever.

I wish Bear was here. He'd sit with me, waiting for Mami Wata. But I know this is something I must do on my own.

Splash. I hold my breath. Is it her?

She nods and water sprays from her hair.

I jump into the dark water, surface, treading water, feeling unafraid. The shore seems hazy, remote. Water feels good.

Wata swims. At ease, I swim beside her. A huge turtle tilts and dives deep beneath me.

Mami Wata pulls me underwater and she breathes glittering bubbles. They're like soda-pop bubbles streaming to me. I swallow them. From the inside, my chest glows.

I breathe like a mermaid.

Wata pulls me toward shore. Gators. I hesitate.

She tugs; my heart races. The gators don't move.

Wata glides to the left, to a pile of logs half in, half out of the water.

I look quickly at the gators on shore, then I look to where Wata's pointing. I see eggs in a nest of damp, blackened twigs and leaves. At least a dozen. Ivory with brown and black specks. They're small, just a third bigger than Sweet Pea's eggs.

The two gators watch us but don't move. Wata waves. One gator's eye blinks.

We swim downstream toward a thicket of cypress trees. Thick trunks rise out of water. Branches arch and leaves on their edges make puffball shapes. Wata points straight up. Another nest. Can't see the eggs, but I bet it's a pelican's nest.

Pay attention. Mami Wata is teaching me.

There's an inlet, a pocket of water. I start searching the grass. Wata smiles. There. Eggs. Round, little
pebbles glimmering with moonlight. One cracks.
Staring, I hold my breath. A webbed foot, then a
green leg. *Crack-crack-crack.* A head pops, a wrinkled
neck extends. A baby turtle!

I sigh, happy, and float on my back. "Thank you,
Wata. I've never seen an egg hatch. Something being
born."

I hear sounds trill, burst staccato then smooth like
a watery echo. Is Wata singing? But then she stops,
her voice becoming sharp, like an irritating alarm.

She lifts her tail, arms outstretched, hands palm-to-
palm; she dives.

I try to follow but I can't kick myself deep enough.

Frustrated, I slap the water. Now the water is
heavy. I'm not graceful. Water is a wall with currents
pushing me upward.

"Wata," I cry. "Wata!"

I'm alone again. Wata is somewhere I can't be. I
swim back toward shore.

Here, I think I hear. Belly-up, Wata's swimming

on her back. She's parallel, just beneath me. I reach.
She reaches.

I'm pulled down, down, down through murky
waters to muddy bottom. There's less and less light.
Then no light. Only Wata's glow.

The glow inside my lungs.

The bottom is like a thick stew. Fat catfish, their
whiskers flicking, rest. Teeny-tiny fish dart, zigzag
through the stringy plants. Wata starts clawing mud;
as soon as she pushes it aside, it slides back.

Her hands move faster and faster. Until, finally, I
see metal pipes, rusty, huge and round.

Oil tunnels. The canals built before the deepwater drills.

Wata lets go of my hand and I float to the surface. My lungs adjust to air.

Grandmère is at the shore, "Maddy!"

"Grandmère!" I shout back.

Arms lifting her dress, feet in the water, Grandmère watches me.

We swim to her. "Grandmère." My feet touch
soil. I stand, dripping water.

"Is she here?" Grandmère whispers.

Gracefully, Wata treads water.

"You don't see her?"

"You mean she's here?" Grandmère asks wonderingly.

"Right there." I point.

Grandmère shakes her head. She can't see Wata swimming right in front of her.

"What does she look like?"

"Young, like me."

"*Non, c'est vrai?* True?"

Mami Wata talks inside my head. "Wata says I see her as Membe saw her. This is how she wanted to appear to me. As a girl."

"You hear her? Understand her? Even my mother couldn't do that," Grandmère marvels. "I've been dreaming of this day. Dreaming you'd see Mami Wata."

"It's sad Membe didn't know about her."

"I think she didn't want to know. She blamed Mami Wata for her enslavement. Sometimes people do that—place blame when they don't know what to do with their grief."

Grandmère walks a couple steps deeper into the water. "Ask her, ask her, Maddy, if she knows me?"

Mami Wata replies; her sounds are beautiful, clear.

"She says, 'I know you. Your mother, your mother before. All of Membe's line.'"

Grandmère weeps happy tears. She drops her hem; it quickly soaks.

Mami Wata leaves, slipping beneath water, leaving no trace.

"Thank you, Mami Wata," Grandmère says. "Thank you for looking after my family."

"Come, Grandmère. Let's go home."

Warm water licks at our feet and ankles. Mud sucks at our toes. Holding her hand, I guide Grandmère home.

Practicing

Clearing my throat, I stand on the porch step like it's a pedestal. I'm practicing telling our story in my own words.

"Capturing slaves was horrible. All of Nature cried. Mami Wata, who so loved Membe, left her African rivers and traveled beside the slave ship through ocean waters to America.

"Even when Membe lost faith, stopped believing in water spirits, Mami Wata stayed loyal, near. Like family. A best friend. Mami Wata made Louisiana her home."

I stop. "How's that, Grandmère? Do you like how I'm saying it? Telling the tale?"

"Very much, Maddy-girl. Water cares for us and we should care for water. Respect nature."

I turn and stare at the beautiful bayou. "Mami Wata is nature's water goddess. But nature is both land and water."

"And air," says Grandmère.

"We've got to be good to both. I mean, all of it—land, water, and air. The whole world."

My teachers would be so proud of me.

"Enslaved, Membe felt lost and abandoned. Stopped believing in magic. Stopped having space inside her mind."

"No imagination."

"She didn't know Mami Wata sent a firefly, a little light inside the dark ship. Like Pandora."

"Who's Pandora?" Grandmère asks.

"I read her story in school. It's a Greek folktale. Pandora was given a box she wasn't supposed to open. But she opened it and all kinds of hateful sprites flew out. Despair. Disease. Maybe even slavery. She cried at how she'd ruined the world. Last, in the bottom of the box, there was a fairy shining bright. Hope. The bright light like Wata's firefly gave hope."

"Sounds like a good tale."

On the porch step, Sweet Pea brushes against me. I stroke her feathers. "Grandmère, do you think Membe would've become sour—"

"Bitter?"

"Yes, bitter. Without the firefly, would Membe have become bitter?"

Thinking, Grandmère rocks.

"You said Membe helped people, her community. If she couldn't have called fireflies would she have been—"

"Different?"

"Oui, Grandmère."

"Come, Maddy-girl." I stand before the rocker. With Grandmère sitting and me standing, we're face-to-face, eye-to-eye.

"Most folks don't know how they're going to react

before hard times come. Hard times do come. It's a part of life. But slavery was the worst hard time.

"Miss Firefly made it easier for Membe to remember herself. To remember self-respect. Giving respect. Helping, healing.

"Though Membe never made peace with Mami Wata, Membe's African values have been passed down to us. Membe's descendants always try to do right."

"The firefly is a symbol of Mami Wata's love."

"Yes. *Oui.*"

"Hope, too." I leap off the steps. "I'm going to name Miss Firefly 'Hope.'"

Sweet Pea ruffles her feathers, clacks.

I raise my hands high. "Come nightfall, I'll call all the fireflies in the world."

Grandmère laughs.

"Mami Wata never abandoned Bon Temps. Mami Wata is a 'Queenie,' too. I've figured it out."

"That's right, Maddy-girl. Finish the story. How does it end?" Air quickens, blowing sea-salt smells from the Gulf. Gray, jagged clouds stream across the sky.

End? Some of my happiness drains. *End?* I remember all the stories I've read. They all have endings. I swallow. Clear my throat again.

"I am Madison Isabelle Lavalier Johnson," I say. "Caller of fireflies." I pause. "Membe's great-great—"

"Great."

"—granddaughter."

"That's part of who you are, Maddy. Not how your story ends."

I'm listening hard to what Grandmère isn't saying. I've connected the dots. Membe to Grandmère to Mami Wata to me.

Grandmère's face is somber. Wistful sad. All Lavalier women are strong. But Grandmère and me are the only ones living who know the truth of Membe's and Mami Wata's tale. We're the only two Lavaliers left to call fireflies. I'm the only one to see the mermaid.

"Who do you want to be?" Grandmère had asked. "A hero," I'd answered.

To be a hero, something bad has to happen.

"Another test," I say. "There's another test."

"*Oui*, Maddy-girl. Another hard time. I've been dreaming about it. Something bad is coming and I don't know what it is."

I shudder.

Hunting for Bear

"I'm going to visit Bear."

"You should wait, Maddy." All morning, Grand-mère's been weeding the garden, staking tomato plants, and picking peas.

All morning, I've been bursting with stories, feelings to share.

"If Bear won't come to me, I'll go to him," I say, feeling bold, not as shy as I once was.

"It's complicated. *He's* complicated. Bear's pa..." Grandmère says. "Bear and his pa have things to work out."

"What things?"

"Complicated things. They need to find their way to simple."

Grandmère pinches thyme, oregano, and parsley. She's going to cook gumbo.

I stroke Sweet Pea. Her feathers bristle like a fan. There's something Grandmère's not saying.

In New Orleans, lots I didn't know. Wasn't much I needed to know.

Eat. Sleep. Go to school. Pay attention to traffic lights, rules. Don't irritate my sisters. Get hugs and kisses from Ma and Pa.

Maybe the whole world is one big puzzle, and I just didn't know it. I only know in the bayou, my feelings are stronger. Sensitive.

I feel—*know*—something's wrong and Grandmère's not telling.

"Grandmère, you said Bear's my best friend on land. Friends see friends. I want to see him. I want to meet his pa."

I want Bear to swim with me and Mami Wata.

But I don't say that. I don't need to say it. Grandmère knows.

"Give me a hug," Grandmère responds. I squeeze her tight, liking how we're both small, just the right size.

Grandmère kisses my forehead. "Holler if you need me, Maddy."

"I'll holler." Then, determined, I walk toward the village, Bear's home. My heart beats hard.

Absence is a sign. Something is wrong with my friend.

"Bear!" I shout, without opening my mouth, hoping he can hear me, *feel* me coming. "Bear? My good friend Bear."

~

"Look who's here," says Old Jake. "Miss Maddy. See my bird?"

A brown pelican rests in his arms. "What's wrong with it?"

"Broken wing."

I try to pet it. The bird snaps, looking at me eagle-eyed.

"Has spirit still," says Old Jake, cradling the bird. "A good sign."

It *is* a sign. Maybe it means there's hurt before things get better?

"Is Bear here?"

Face grim, gold tooth sparkling, Jake points. "Down the way. Last house on the left."

Charlotte and Ben beg me to play. "Later," I say. I wave to Mister Cochon. He's on his porch rocking, a straw hat on his head. Jolene sews.

None of the grown-ups stop me. Funny—as I get closer to Bear's house, I wish they would.

~

Boat engines, a broken mast, bicycle rims, and fishing poles clutter the yard. Chickens peck at dirt. They're not like Sweet Pea. They're busy, heads down, paying no attention to me.

Bear's house is on stilts, run-down gray, looking like it might fall over. Mold and marsh grass line and hang from the shack's bottom.

Except for the chicks, it doesn't look like anybody lives here. No Bear calling "Come on." No pa doing chores. Just a deserted old shack with a gash in its tin roof.

I climb the steps. Peek through the window. Dust is everywhere. The stove's dirty. Dried food sits on plates. In the middle of the floor, there's a duffel bag with men's clothes spilling out. A man—on a cot, chest bare, jeans on, an arm dangling, scraping the floor—snores.

Where's Bear?

I search the small square. No Bear. I push my head farther, and look down. Beneath the window, legs to his chest, hands beneath his head, Bear sleeps.

"Bear?"

He starts. Sits up, scared.

"You okay?"

He quickly glances at the cot. "Shhh." He presses his fingers to his lips.

I step back. Bear comes out, waving me to follow.

160

*   *   *

Round back, there's a hen pen, a shed, and a canoe, turned upside down on dry land.

Bear's a mess, his face and clothes dirty, his hair matted. He doesn't smile, doesn't seem happy to see me. He sweats in a denim long-sleeved shirt. This isn't the Bear I know.

"I miss you."

"Pa'll be gone soon."

"I want to meet him."

"Pa doesn't like company." Bear picks up a rock, hurling it. "Doesn't like anything."

"You said, 'He's the best pa. Strongest, smartest.'"

"He is, he is." Bear's not crying but his gaze darts wild—house, forest, sky. Back to the house. He throws another rock.

"He was the best pa. Took me fishing. Hiking. Hunting."

"Bear." I clutch his arm.

He winces. I let go. He won't look at me.

"Bear?" I reach for his arm again. He backs away. It doesn't make sense in this heat to wear a long-sleeved shirt. I step closer. "Show me your arm, Bear."

"Go, Maddy."

"Won't."

"You're not wanted here, Maddy. Go on home."

Shoulders slouched, Bear seems small. Not brave. Not my adventurous friend.

"Bear!" It's an awful roar. "Bear, where the hell are you? Bear!"

Bear starts trembling. "Go, Maddy. Just go."

"I'm not leaving."

"Bear." Bear's pa staggers round. He's muscular, thick, and furious. "What did I tell you about sneaking out?"

"I didn't, Pa."

"Sneaking away. What? Trying to find your ma? She's gone. Gone." He keeps lumbering, hands swiping at Bear.

Bear ducks.

"You're not going anywhere." Spittle specks his mouth and beard. He lurches. "You won't go."

Bear doesn't move quickly enough. His pa grips his arm. Bear howls. His pa frowns but he doesn't let go.

"Leave Bear alone. Let him go." I pull Bear's pa's arm.

"Who're you?" he roars.

Bear keeps screaming. I dig in with my feet, tugging his arm like a tug-of-war rope. The arm won't budge.

Bear's twisting, trying to cut loose. His face is puckered with pain.

I kick. Kick again. Bear's pa staggers, lets go of Bear.

Bear falls in the dirt.

His pa rubs his shin.

"Leave my friend alone. You're hurting him." I'm breathing hard, fighting back tears. "Bully," I shout.

Another roar, then a ferocious wail. Bear's pa lunges, stumbles toward me.

"Pa," Bear shouts. "Pa!" Bear leaps onto his father's back, his arms wrapped about his neck.

I should run. I know I should, but I keep still. Bear and his pa twist, turn. Bear keeps hold while his pa tries to pull him off.

"You're being mean. Bear loves you. And you've hurt him. That's just mean. Mean, mean, mean."

With each "mean," Bear's pa staggers like I've hit him with a frying pan. He falls to his knees. Bear slides off his back.

Bear's pa shakes his head, his whole body like he's having a nightmare, like he's trying to wake up.

He's confused, I think. Another kind of sleep-walking.

"I'm not going nowhere, Pa. Promise," Bear says, hurried, intent. "Not going nowhere. Nowhere. Maddy's my friend. I'm not going nowhere. Promise. Pa," he says, shrill, shouting. "I promise. Promise."

Bear's pa covers his face. His fingers are scratched, scarred, stained with oil.

Bear pats his pa, comforting. He's got his arm around his waist like he's supporting him. "It's all right, Pa. It's all right."

I'm confused. Unashamed, Bear's pa drops his hands and cries. I've never seen a grown man cry. His blue eyes fill and tears fall onto his cheeks, beard. He doesn't even wipe his face.

"You're not going to leave me, too?"

"No, Pa. I'm not going to leave you." Bear is comforting, helping him to stand.

Bear's pa's face is craggy, sorrowful. He coughs and I step back, smelling alcohol. Bear turns red. He's embarrassed that I'm meeting his pa.

Bear tugs, "Come on, Pa."

"I need a beer."

"Food," I say.

"Who're you, again?" Bear's pa asks, not sarcastic, just puzzled.

I don't answer, just trail behind as Bear leads his big, powerful pa by the hand.

❧

Bear's pa sleeps while me and Bear make stew. Quiet, we work. Bear fills the pot with water. I add beans.

Mostly that's all there is in the cupboard, beans and a bag of rice.

No wonder Bear likes eating at Grandmère's.

I cut an old, sprouting onion. Bear pinches salt, pepper, and rosemary into rolling, boiling water.

"There's probably vegetables on the porch."

"On the porch?"

"Liza leaves pickings from her garden."

Outside, I find a basket with tomatoes and okra. I lift a bottle of hot sauce.

"That's Mister Cochon. He leaves hot sauce."

The basket is a kind gift, but it's sad Bear needs to rely on it.

There's a soft knock on the screen door. "Mister Jake?" He pushes a brown paper bag into my hand. "A bit of chicken thigh. Don't tell my birds," he says. He looks at Bear. "Your pa better?"

" 'Bout the same."

As if he knows in his sleep we are talking about him, Bear's pa grunts, turns on his side snoring.

"Thank you, Mister Jake," I say, closing the screen door.

*　　*　　*

At the stove, Bear puts a lid on the pot. He doesn't look at me. "They always do that. Bring me food. Even Pa's got to eat."

I gently touch Bear's sleeve. "Do they know?"

He winces. "Pa's not beating me."

"You're supposed to tell if a grown-up hurts you."

"It's not like that."

"You wouldn't even have to tell Grandmère. She'd know. Oh…" I breathe. "That's why you haven't been coming around."

"That and Pa won't let me."

"Oh, Bear." Bear's been hurting while I've been happy.

Embarrassed, his face flushes.

"I'll wash the celery, tomato. You add the chicken?"

Bear nods, but he doesn't look at me.

His pa snores. The kettle top, not a tight fit, rattles. I chop vegetables.

"Ready?" asks Bear.

"Ready." With a pot holder, Bear lifts the lid. Carrots,

celery, and onion slide off the cutting board. Bear drops in the crinkly pink chicken thigh.

"Hot sauce now or later?"

"Later," answers Bear, settling the lid. He still won't look at me.

I start washing dishes.

"Pa's scared," Bear whispers. "Scared I'll go. It's Ma's fault."

I turn.

"No, don't," says Bear. "Don't look at me. I'm ashamed."

I want to hug Bear and tell him he's the one wronged. I don't think he'd listen. I keep washing dishes.

"Me and Pa went fishing. Caught fat redfish. Came home and Ma was just gone. Not a trace. No comb, no clothes. Not even a hairpin.

"Just her smell left. Night-blooming jasmine. She had a little bottle of perfume."

I sniff. The house is stale. Bare and dirty.

"Pa went wild. Started drinking. When he comes

home from the rig, he gets sick all over again. Drinks too much. Thinks I'm going to leave, too."

"You wouldn't," I say, certain, turning.

"No, I wouldn't. Oh, Maddy, he holds and holds me. Tight. Hard. Sometimes I can't get away 'til he sleeps. He holds and holds. Cries and won't let my arm go."

I look at his covered arms. "Oh, Bear, let me see." Bear's head hangs.

I dry my hands, unbutton Bear's cuff. "Let me see.

"It's not your fault. Not your fault at all," I chatter, rolling the denim.

Bear's skin is bruised, purple and black; his wrist and elbow are swollen. I'm sad, sorry for him. I should've visited sooner. I haven't been a good friend at all.

City Maddy wouldn't know what to do. But I do.

"Sassafras. I'll be back." I go outside and peel slivers of bark. Inside, I mix it with water, pounding it into a paste.

I soap the dishrag. Wring it clean. Then, with a knife, I smooth sassafras paste.

*　　*　　*

"Sit." I wrap the rag about Bear's arm.

Bear closes his eyes. I know the cool paste makes his arm feel better. I tuck the rag so it won't unravel.

"Bear? Where're you? Bear?" we hear. His pa is stirring.

Bear starts to rise.

I stop him. "He's getting his arm fixed."

Bear's pa rubs his eyes. "Who're you?"

I don't answer.

His feet hit the floor. "My head hurts."

He lifts a pitcher of water next to the cot and drinks.

Bear watches, wary. "Made stew, Pa."

"Smells good." He tries to walk steady toward the table and chairs.

"Who're you again?"

"I'm Maddy."

He sits at the table like nothing happened. Like he hadn't acted wild. Or hurt Bear. He strokes his beard, down to the tip. His hair is a rough black, like steel wool, but his eyes are blue and twinkling. I don't understand how now he seems like a young Santa Claus.

"What's on your arm, boy?"

Me and Bear look at each other. "Nothin'," says Bear.

I unwrap the rag.

Bear's pa is shocked. He touches Bear's fingers, stares at the blue-black thumbprints and circles.

"Did I do this?"

"You didn't mean to."

Standing, Bear's pa lifts Bear in the biggest, gentlest hug. He holds and holds him, saying, "I'm sorry, I'm sorry, I'm sorry. Won't drink. Won't hurt you again."

Weeping drains out of Bear, loud at first, then whimpering to a thin whistle. Like he's been holding in the sound for years. It's not words but sounds vibrating that tell how much he misses his pa, his ma, and how much he loves them both.

I hear how he's been frightened and lonely. I also hear shame.

I hear how hard it's been for Bear to pretend nothing was wrong.

I tiptoe away, gently closing the screen door. Outside is flourishing with damp heat and the color green.

I should help Grandmère season the gumbo. I think we'll have company for dinner.

I'm still worried. I'll tell Grandmère Bear and his pa are trying to get to simple. I hope they make it.

Mending

On the porch, me and Grandmère wait for Bear and his pa. She's rocking. I'm sitting on the steps, staring down the path into the forest.

Inside, the table is set for four. The kerosene lamps are lit.

"Do you think they'll know to come?"

"They'll know," says Grandmère, leaning forward, the rocker creaking. "You did a good thing, Maddy. Looked after your friend."

"Wish I'd gone sooner."

"It was just the right time. You did it. Did what was in your heart."

"How come you didn't go?"

"I did. Many times. All Bon Temps folks did. Told to go away. We made sure they were fed. Took extra care of Bear when his pa was gone.

"Thought it was loneliness. Grief. Thought Bailey, Bear's pa, would heal with time. Didn't guess Bear was being harmed and not telling."

Grandmère pauses. The rocker stops creaking. "We all—all of us should've paid better attention."

"Bear says his pa didn't mean it."

"Doesn't make it right. Glad you were here to catch it, Maddy. Shame on me for not."

I scoot close, pat-patting her shoulder. "You said, 'Do good and it'll fly right back to you.' Everybody in Bon Temps tries to do good. I'm trying to do good, too.

"We'll all keep doing good, won't we Grandmère? Best we can."

Grandmère's eyes fill with tears but they don't fall like Bear's pa's.

"I've got sayings, too," I say.

"You do? Do tell."

"Hugs are good medicine."

"*Vrai*," she laughs. "Smart, smart, Maddy-girl."

We hug and hug and hug some more. Grand-mère's bones relax.

"I've got another one. Another saying. 'Planting seeds grows happiness.'"

"*C'est vrai*." Grandmère starts rocking again, her lips upturned.

I think but don't say: *Sometimes bad happens.*

Sayings come from observing the world. As true as the sun rises and sets, bad *is*. That's what I've learned.

Oil and salt destroy land. A bird's wing gets broken. A turtle gets eaten by a gator.

Mami Wata couldn't stop Membe being captured as a slave.

Over Grandmère's shoulder, I see my firefly. A tiny lamp in the dark.

I see Bear. "Bear!" I shout, spinning, leaping onto the ground. Bear bobs his head, grinning.

Bear's pa is clean cut. His face is wrinkled, sun-washed but smooth, pink-skinned where his beard had been. He wears denim and a cotton tee. Muscles bulge up and down his shoulders and arms. His eyes, though, are red-rimmed and showing red veins.

Gently, he shakes my hand, sandwiching it between both of his. "I should've known you were Queenie's kin.

"You've got a good kick."

"You kicked him?" Grandmère asks. "Not sure that's kindness, Maddy."

"Don't scold, Queenie. I needed that kick. Look what I was doing. Show her, Bear."

Bear holds out his arm, pushes up his sleeve, and unwraps his bandage.

Grandmère stares. She doesn't say anything. Anger tightens every part of her body.

Bear's pa looks sick, like he's going to throw up. "I'm shamed, Queenie."

"You didn't mean it," argues Bear.

"Doesn't matter. You deserve better, Bear. You're a good son."

Bear likes his pa's words, I can tell.

"I shouldn't kick. I'm sorry, too, Mister—"

"Bailey. Just plain Bailey," he says, "and you're Maddy, Bear's new friend."

"Best friend," Bear says. I smile, grateful.

"Let's eat," says Grandmère. "Bailey, next time you hurt Bear, I'll kick you, too."

We smile, uneasy.

Even though Bailey tried to clean himself up, he squints like the light pains him. I think he's still a bit drunk. Bear starts eating, one-handed, his sore arm on his lap. Even though we ate afternoon stew, he's trying to eat as much as he can. He's hungry. Every few bites, he looks across at his pa.

Hunched, Bailey eats slow. He mumbles, not looking at any of us, just talking to his bowl of gumbo. "I'll try to be a better pa."

Louisiana Shrimp Boat

Bailey, Bear's pa, hollers, "Come on! Time's a'wasting."
Shaggy-haired, his voice hearty, sun sparkling behind
him, standing tall on the white boat, Bailey does look
and sound like a grown-up Bear.

"Come on, Maddy." Bear's pulling my hand,
making me run faster. Not even dawn and we're
sweaty, faces flushed.

We're going on an adventure.

"Ya-hoo," Bear and I shout. Both running strong,
happy. Eager for shrimping.

I've eaten Louisiana shrimp. Cooked them. But I've never seen them harvested.

The boat, white, maybe fourteen feet long, sits deep in the water. On each side, it has huge black mesh draped like butterfly wings. It looks like it could lift off and fly.

Getting closer, I see the wings are really nets—layers of sloping folds hanging from metal cables and poles. Thick ropes lock the boat in place.

"Mind the gap," says Bailey.

Bear climbs the slant plank, reaches for his pa, and jumps over the ledge into the boat.

"Come on, Maddy!" Bear and his pa shout. I laugh, racing up the plank. Bailey grabs my waist and swings me high. My heart races. My shoes touch the deck.

I sigh, thrilled. This is going to be a good day.

Bolden is in the pilot's cabin. From below, Willie Mae pokes her head.

"Where's Charlotte? Ben and Douglass?" I ask.

"Cochon's watching them. Says we owe him a shrimp boil."

"Got enough ice, Willie Mae?" asks Bailey.

"Tons in the hold."

Bolden starts the engine. You can smell oil burning. Willie Mae undoes the mooring ties.

Bailey helps me and Bear into life vests.

He squats before me. I like how he looks straight into my eyes.

"Water is wonderful. But got to respect its power." His finger taps my nose. "How'd Queenie and Mother Water feel if you had an accident, fell overboard, and drowned?"

I gulp. "You know Mami Wata?"

"I know all the old-time tales. Queenie tells everybody."

"Have you seen her?"

Bailey rises. "I figure I'll see her when I see Santa Claus."

"Do you know about the firefly? Mami Wata sent her to Membe."

Bailey scratches his head. "I've heard the tale. Seen fireflies. But fireflies don't live in Africa."

No wonder he's sad. He's lost magic, imagination. What about other folks?

I feel sure Ma knows Mami Wata is real. Even if she hasn't seen her.

My sisters wouldn't believe in Mami Wata even if they saw her.

Bear looks at me funny. I sit on the boat's edge, staring at the lapping water between the dock and the boat.

Slowly, the boat backs up. Bailey's foot keeps it from scraping the dock.

"Clear!" Bailey and Willie Mae periodically shout. Except for the dock, I can't see much in the way—just water. Then, both holler, "All clear."

"Coming about!" Bolden yells, turning the wheel, making the boat pivot and head out to the Gulf.

The engine fires, pops like a firecracker. The boat put-putters, passing the airboat, a canoe, and another shrimp boat with a hole in its side.

"What you thinking?" Bear scoots beside me.

"Nothing."

"Tell me, Maddy."

"Can't."

Nose down, his eyes peer into mine. "You'll blink first."

Both of us stare. "I can see it," says Bear.

"See what?"

"See you thinking too hard, hiding. If you weren't hiding something, you'd blink."

I blink like crazy.

"Too late. You tried too hard to show you weren't thinking."

"I want to show you, not tell you. Not here, Bear."

Bear looks more relaxed.

Patience. Eleven means patient, Grandmère said. And because Bear's so patient, I cup my hands over his ear and whisper, "I found her, Bear. The girl in the water. She's a mermaid."

I lean back. Bear's face is shining.

"You believe me?"

"I do. Always did."

"Maddy, Bear, come see," Bailey calls.

Bear wants to ask me a thousand questions.

Cheeks red, he clenches his hands, hops, and sucks in his lips, trying to keep his mouth still.

"Maddy? Bear?"

"Later, Bear, I promise. I'll tell you everything."

We walk the deck, careful of the nets. They're steel wire, not at all delicate up close.

"Louisiana paradise," Bailey says proudly. "Traveling in the Gulf."

It's a different beauty than the wetlands—rolling, blue-green waters, not heavy and brackish with clumps of moss. The sun makes a sheen across the endless water. Foaming crests sparkle. A cool breeze sweeps.

"Salt. Do you smell it?"

"I do, Pa," says Bear.

"Me, too."

Bear and I smile. We've got a secret. The secret makes the day, the boat ride, sweeter.

⁓

Topside, the boat slices through blue-green water. Underneath is another world.

Except for Bolden driving, we're all quiet. Bailey and Bear sit. Willie Mae lies flat, sunning. I hold on to the mast.

I like this. The wind blowing, the sun rising, and the clanking of the nets. The puttering of the motor. No chatter.

Bailey, Bolden, and Willie Mae are different from my ma and pa. Like Grandmère is different. They're at home in the bayou. Couldn't be city people.

"What's that?" It looks like an ugly scratch on the horizon. A looming speck.

Bailey's expression is grim. "Where I work. Deep-water oil rig."

"Told Maddy all about it," says Bear. "Told her it was your other home. Told her you don't like it. Like the bayou better."

"All true."

"I'll get binoculars."

Bailey grunts as Bear goes.

"Do you hate it?"

"Do and don't. It's complicated. Drilling is dangerous. But necessary. If I don't do it, someone else will. Folks need jobs. World needs oil."

I feel the boat shudder. Bolden has shut off the engine.

"Let's see," says Bear, excited. "Come on." Carrying the binoculars, he pulls Bolden. "I rarely see where Pa lives when he's not with me."

"I'll focus," says Bolden, his baseball cap backward, squinting with one eye. He twists the dials. "There. Guests first."

He hands me the binoculars. At first, all I see is fuzzy water.

"Higher," says Bolden. "Higher and an inch to the left."

A concrete house on stilts. Two black towers of crisscrossing metal. Red rails. A huge crane.

"Let me see!"

I hand the binoculars to Bear. "It's huge."

"Where do you sleep, Pa?"

"Bunks are belowdeck."

"Like a slave ship?"

"Not at all. We've got nice quarters, a rec room. We get paid. But sometimes, when it's dark, when you hear folks breathing, shifting in their sleep, it feels suffocating.

"You get up. Go out. Want to see the stars, feel the wind, not pumped air. Want to hear waves lapping. Folks get lonely, disoriented."

"Any women?"

"Sometimes, Maddy. But not on this rig."

"What are the towers for?"

"Drill bits. Thousand tons of force."

"You can't see them," Bolden grunts. "Can't see the pounding, the harm done to the ocean floor.

"How far down. Pa? How far?"

"Miles and miles down. So far down there isn't light, only blackness and freezing cold. Drill bits hit bottom, then go a mile deeper, sucking crude oil. Electric pumps move it to the surface."

"It must sound awful in the water," I say. Screeching, churning, all day, all night.

"Wonder how far the sound carries?" asks Willie Mae, standing behind me and Bear.

"If I were a fish, I'd stay as far away as I could," says Bear.

"Or a mermaid," I murmur.

"What?"

"Nothing, Willie Mae. Just muttering."

"Well, at least they're not tearing up Bon Temps anymore," says Willie Mae.

"Why'd they stop?" I ask.

"Queenie and others told tales of what the bayou used to be like. Showed folks the damage. Acres of land that disappeared."

"Grandmère helped get the drilling to stop?"

"Some think so. But I think it was business. Plain and simple," says Bolden. "There's more oil deeper out. More money to be made."

Willie Mae pats her husband's back. Bear and his pa stand side by side. I think Bear wants his pa to hug him but, maybe, he's too afraid.

Bailey, Bear, Bolden, and Willie Mae—Bon Temps people. They're scared. Looking out to sea, frowning at the rig.

I look through the binoculars again.

"How much oil?"

"Eighty thousand gallons a day. It's called *crude* first. When it's processed, refined, it becomes oil folks can use."

"How much oil does the world need?"

"Millions of gallons. Maybe billions. There're rigs all over the world. Some drill deeper."

When the crude's gone, will the earth dry up, dry out, pucker like a raisin? I want to ask the grown folks, but they're grim, staring at the rig like it's a big blot on the blue sea.

"Here." Willie Mae passes out mugs.

"You, too, Maddy. More milk, but a little coffee, too. Nothing like something warm for comfort."

Bolden gulps his coffee, then shouts, "Let's shrimp. Enjoy what we have. While we can. Let's go. Shrimping time."

Shrimp Party

Shrimping is fun.

Bolden and Bailey work the pulleys, and on both sides of the boat, the mesh nets come down and sink into the water. Willie Mae counts the time and when she's ready, she shouts, "Rise!"

Up, up come the nets. Some hauls are fair, some good. This one is GREAT. Rushing seawater drains from the nets. "Pull!" shouts Bolden. He and Bailey make the nets move inward, over the deck. Water sprays everything. Me and Bear giggle, already soaked.

The nets burst with shrimp, wriggling like over-size brown bugs.

"Open!" me and Bear squeal, and Bolden and Bailey make the nets spring wide. Thousands of shrimp tumble down and out.

I never knew shrimp had fanned tails, three pairs of legs, long antennae, and bulging black eyes. In the store, shrimp are frozen-white and curled like a C.

Here, seeing them flop on deck makes you wonder how such funny pink creatures can taste so good.

Me and Bear start hollering. "Thank you!" "Thank you!" "Thank you so much!"

"Who you thanking?" asks Willie Mae, handing me a wide broom.

"The shrimp. Like Sweet Pea giving us eggs for eating, I'm thanking the shrimp for the goodness they'll give us."

"You sound like Queenie." Then, she tells Bailey and Bolden, "Thank the shrimp. Thank them for gumbo. Jambalaya. Shrimp étouffée. Shrimp and grits. Barbecued shrimp. Boiled shrimp. Thank them for the—what did you say, Maddy?"

"For the goodness they'll give us."

"The goodness they'll give us," echoes Bear.

"Thank you, thank you," everyone calls as we sweep and sweep the shrimp into the ice-filled hold.

Wearing gloves, me and Bear check corners and beneath ropes, and pluck shrimp still caught in the net. Not a single shrimp is forgotten.

Soaking wet, our arms, legs, and backs aching, everyone's happy.

"Bear," calls Bailey. "Come here." Bailey tousles Bear's hair and gives him a wet, sloppy hug. Pleased, Bear, eyes closed on his pa's chest, hugs back.

Bolden, grinning, says, "Close the hatch. Time to head home."

Me and Willie Mae snap the locks in place. The engine chugs to life. More sun, wind, salt, and shrimp smells. Pelicans and swallows swoop low, sniffing our boat, searching for spare shrimp.

~⌒

Bailey, Bolden, and Willie Mae are in the cabin. Laughter floats out. Bailey talks about "good eating."

Bolden crows, "Shrimping and the bayou belong together. Like white on rice."

Bear and I sit on cushions, staring over the side into blue water. We're quiet. My bones are tired. I feel good. Tonight, I'll introduce Bear to Mami Wata.

~⌒

"Look, Maddy. A dolphin."

"Where?"

"There."

I gaze where Bear's pointing. A few waves out, there's a shadow gliding, keeping pace with the boat.

"Hope it jumps."

"Me, too." I see the tail flap up, down. It changes course, swimming ever closer to the boat. I squint. Light reflecting off the waves makes it hard to see.

Its upper body seems more brown than gray. Long black strands—seaweed?—fan back and sideways.

"Probably a bottlenose." The shadow disappears. "It's gone now. Too bad it didn't jump." Bear sits, cross-legged, on deck.

Kneeling, I lean farther and farther over the boat's side. The shadow appears again, swimming closer and closer. I think it might be Wata.

I stretch my hand.

A hand reaches upward. Fingertips touch. I see black eyes.

I squeal and fall back on Bear. "Whoa!" he gasps, steadying me.

"You kids all right?" yells Bailey, poking his head out of the cabin.

"We're fine," I say.

"What's wrong, Maddy?"

Breathing heavy, I say, "Secret, Bear. I saw another mermaid."

Scrambling up, clutching the boat's ledge, Bear asks, "Where, Maddy? Where?"

"There. Don't you see her? You saw her shadow before."

Bear stares ever so hard, searching the sun-streaked ocean. "I don't see anything," he says sadly.

"She's there."

I see silver, not rainbow scales. A face lighter brown than black. Black eyes, pink lips. Unsmiling, she swims back and forth, like she's pacing beside the boat.

Dumbstruck, I shake my head. "She's not Mami Wata."

"You mean there're more? More mermaids?"

"Hello," I call. But I don't hear sounds back.

"Look!" I shout. "Another mermaid!"

"Where?"

"And another," I point right.

"I don't see anything," Bear complains. "Not even a shadow."

"You believe me, don't you?" It's important that Bear believes me.

"I believe you, Maddy."

The mermaids keep pace with the boat. "Grand-mère couldn't see them, either."

"If Queenie couldn't see them, I surely won't. What do they look like, Maddy?" Bear asks, good-natured, excited.

"One has black eyes and silver scales. This one, treading right here, has tan skin and white hair. All three seem young." I pause. Three.

"The third one, Maddy. What does she look like?"

My throat feels dry. "Her scales are bright blue. She's wearing a circle of yellow flowers on her head."

"I've bet they're beautiful."

"They are." *Heartache comes in threes.* But I can't believe these mermaids mean harm.

All three raise their arms. They seem to be embracing the whole sky.

Their arms lower, and they point to the horizon. I search the distance, the invisible line from their fingers, through air, stretching to where water meets sky. And then I spot it.

A thin, black line like someone took a felt marker and drew. And drew. And drew.

The line thickens.

Scared, I remember my dream.

Black ink—no, crude—spreads like a thick blanket over the water.

Panicked, I shake Bear's arm. "Do you see? Do you see?"

"Shhh, Maddy, shhh." Patting my back, Bear tries to comfort me.

"I'm not crazy, Bear."

"Never thought you were."

Mermaids. Blackening water. I'm not sure what it means. Water laps against the boat; crests of foam rise and fall. "The mermaids are gone," I whisper, my voice catching.

Washed with sunlight, the sea sparkles blue again.

Motorboating, hearing whiffs of grown-ups' chatter, smelling sea and shrimp, the day seems happy. But, trembling, I slump on the deck.

Something bad is going to happen.

Quiet, Bear sits beside me. He's patient.

"I did see a shadow, Maddy. That must mean something."

"Yes, Bear."

But my dream stays with me.

Something bad will happen.

Absence

The Gulf of Mexico is so beautiful. It swishes with white-tipped waves. Bailey climbs into a motorboat that taxis him away toward the rig. Farther and farther out to sea, Bailey looks smaller and smaller as the motorboat bounces, slices, and cuts through salt water. Bear climbs a tree and waves. Grandmère walks home.

I keep watch long after I can't see the boat, searching the horizon for new signs.

Being brave is hard. New things happen all the time—like coming to the bayou, meeting Grandmère and Bear, swimming with Mami Wata.

Will I be brave enough to make it through to my story's end?

Three nights pass. Nothing happens.

Beside me, on the porch, Bear snores. Inside the cottage, Grandmère sleeps. I hope she's having happy dreams.

I can't sleep. The wood slats are too hard. A mosquito bites. My mind won't rest. I keep dreaming of darkness covering water.

I walk round to Sweet Pea's shed. She's sleeping, her pointy beak and head tucked beneath her wing. She's warming eggs. Sweet Pea's going to be a momma.

The half-moon is more yellow than white tonight. It doesn't look right. I sniff. Instead of smelling of life, tonight the bayou smells sour, like dead fish. I hug my knees. *Heartache comes in threes.* Even if it's mermaids?

A bird with a crooked wing means sorrow. Old Jake's bird was broken and crooked.

I bite my nails. If I were home, I'd be reading a

book, hiding from my sisters. Or maybe I'd be helping Ma cook gumbo?

Sweet Pea opens her eyes. She's telling me to rest.

"'Night, Sweet Pea. I can't wait to see your chicks."

I turn, slow.

Bushes and leaves make long, crooked shadows.
When I listen hard, the bayou is filled with chirps,
cracklings, and stirrings of small creatures. To my
left, a rabbit hops, its head tilting left, then right. Its
teeth munch grass. I wonder if this gray-brown rabbit was born this spring?

I crouch, watching the rabbit eat. Fluffy fur.
Long pointy ears. Black eyes.

The rabbit sees me. It doesn't run.

I gasp. *Mami Wata is swimming, pointing at fire.
Huge, towering flames rise from the ocean, licking the sky. In
the air, smoke billows; in the water, there are swirling webs of
black.*

Mami Wata looks terrified. She covers her eyes.

I run. "Bear, wake up. We need to get to the
water."

"I'm tired, Maddy. Let me sleep." Damp hair

sticks to his forehead. Part of me wants to let Bear sleep, but I need to go. Now.

"You have to drive Mister Cochon's airboat."

"He'll skin me for sure."

"Bear. We must!" I don't tell him how confused I am. Doesn't water put out fire? "Please, Bear."

He jumps up, slips his feet into his shoes. "Let's go."

I leap off the porch, half running. Grandmère should sleep, I decide. Stay happy dreaming as long as she can.

My feet move faster and faster. Bear is right beside me, picking up speed, panting.

~

Even with headlights, riding through pitch-black dark is frightening. Bear doesn't gun the airboat's engine. He steers carefully, slowly.

"Hurry." I squirm, barely able to keep still.

"Don't want to hit a log. Or a gator."

"I know, Bear." But I don't tell him I'm afraid of what I don't know. Where's Mami Wata? Not seeing her makes me more afraid. Where're the fireflies?

201

"Here." Bear leaps off the boat and ties it to the wharf. My feet crunch sand. I look right, left. The stretch of beach is lovely, calm. There's nothing wrong.

"You okay, Maddy?"

"I don't know." With the Gulf and sky both dark, its impossible to see the horizon. I feel like I'm at the end of the world.

The water *whooshes*. The waves barely lap the shore.

"Listen." It's a low rumbling sound, like shifting earth, sand. An earthquake?

"I don't hear anything, Maddy."

"It's coming. It's getting louder. Don't you hear it, Bear?" *It's coming*, I think. The bad is coming.

The rumbling, groans, growls—louder and louder, like a train racing too fast on a track. Then, *bam*, *boom*. Explosions, like bombs being dropped in the distance.

"There." I point at the far left horizon.

Just like my vision—flames, yellow and orange, lick the sky.

Flames spiral higher and higher, like a towering candle. *It's beautiful*, I think. Bright colors against the black night.

But I don't understand how there can be a fire in the ocean. How flames, fierce as a giant torch, can burn and burn and burn on the horizon.

"The rig!" Bear shouts. His face is twisted, ugly-sad. "Pa? Pa!"

I didn't think. The oil rig is on fire.

Bear kicks off his shoes, runs, then dives into the water.

"Stop. Stop, Bear. Please stop." Scrambling forward, I kick off my shoes, too.

Water is up to my chest. I dive, swimming after Bear, who's pulling faster and farther away.

I can't see him, only the splash his body makes.

I'm not used to swimming in the sea. Bear's the stronger swimmer. I'll never reach him.

I think: *Bailey's dead*. I don't want to believe it, but I somehow know. And Bear might drown swimming out to sea.

I swim hard, harder than I've ever swum before.

I'm a mermaid, I tell myself. I don't need to breathe. My legs are powerful like a tail, propelling me. My arms are quick, slapping strong. Water knows to move out of my way.

I swim.

I see Bear's feet, his billowy pants. I reach . . . and catch his ballooning shirt. I grip it tight. I kick and clutch with both hands.

Bear jerks, shouting, screaming, "Let me go. Let me go!" We're both coughing, swallowing water. Struggling, we're off-balance, pushing each other under. Salt stings our eyes. We're both gasping. "Let me go." Bear heaves forward, submerging both of us. His foot kicks my shoulder. My arm hits his head. We're both going to drown.

I let go. I have to.

Bear swims toward the distant fire.

"Bear!" I scream, gasping, treading water. "Come back. I can't swim as good as you."

"I've got to save Pa."

"You can't. The fire is miles away."

"I can."

"You can't."

Bear lifts and falls with the waves. Currents are pulling us farther apart.

"Help me, Bear. I don't swim as well as you."

His hair is wet and plastered, his checkered shirt puffed, the collar tangled about his throat. Flames spike into the sky.

I need Bear to understand what I'm saying. I need him to want to save me. Otherwise, he might never come back.

Bear stops swimming and floats.

I keep quiet. There's nothing to say. His pa is dead. Waves, one after another, rock us. We're drifting farther from shore. If we get too far out, neither of us will have the strength.

There's a splash, a shadow gliding by me. Mami Wata? It has to be, I decide. I know Mami Wata wouldn't let me drown. But what about Bear?

In the Gulf, flames keep glowing, steady and strong.

"I need you, Bear. I can't make it back without you."

He keeps floating, giving no sign that he hears me.

"I need you to help me."

Bear lifts his head, flips, and swims to me. He grabs my hand. "All right, Maddy. I'll help you."

Bear is saving me.

And I am saving Bear.

Healing

Grandmère tucks Bear into my bed. She gives him hugs and sassafras tea, and as he cries, she sings him to sleep.

I feel useless and sad.

Come morning, Mister Cochon visits our shack. He stands near the table, too miserable to sit. He says, "Oil explosion. The deepwater rig. Nine men missing, two found dead."

"Pa?" asks Bear, lying on the cot. His eyes are rimmed red with shadows.

I can see Mister Cochon wants to lie. To say Bear's pa is still missing.

"He's dead, Bear. I'm sorry."

Bear slides back the roped sheet to hide.

I pat Mister Cochon's hand. "Bear knew," I say. "He already knew."

How to explain Bear was hoping beyond hope? Wanting the impossible.

~

For two days, firefighting boats battle the blaze with dynamite and water.

"Dynamite blows flames away from oil," says Bolden. "Like blowing out a candle. No oil to feed on, water can put the fire out."

It is awful watching Bear tremble uncontrollably each time he hears the dynamite explosions. Hands about my knees, I sit near his feet and cry. Grand-mère keeps him warm and puts bundles of thyme, for strength, beneath his pillow.

The oil-rig fire is a hard candle to blow out.

Sunday, the third day since his pa died, Bear eats breakfast with us. Pancakes. Three slices of ham. Then, without saying a word, he lies back on the cot again, sliding the sheet shut.

It is good seeing Bear eat, but I don't eat much. I'm too worried.

"There's more to come," I say, softly. "More that I dreamed."

"What do you mean, Maddy-girl?"

I look at the curtain, knowing behind it Bear is tangled in sheets, but I don't know if he's asleep or awake.

"On the porch," I say, and Grandmère follows me. I hold tight to the rail.

"I don't understand."

"Me, neither, Grandmère. I dreamed the fire. But I dreamed more."

"Like what?"

"Spiders spitting, spinning oil. A black line, growing bigger and bigger, covering the Gulf.

"It isn't over, Grandmère. It's not the end."

Grandmère strokes my cheek. "Sometimes we just have to bear the hard times."

I don't want to bear it, I think. I want all the unhappiness to go away.

"I didn't know Bear's pa was going to die," I blurt.

"Sometimes dreams, visions don't show all there is to know."

"Too many mysteries, Grandmère."

"You'll puzzle it out. Won't you, Maddy?" Grandmère is worn out, her shoulders slumped. She's worried, grieving, too.

"I will," I say.

I walk south.

The air isn't fresh anymore. Gusts of wind bring smells of burnt, simmering crude. Black specks float in the air. I don't want to see the Gulf. My head hurts. What's going to happen?

"Hey, Maddy. Help me cook."

"Hey, Mister Cochon." His cheer makes me smile. "What you cooking?"

"Whatever you want. Keep me and you busy. Maybe get Bear to eat."

"He's had pancakes. Ham."

"Good for Bear. Got to keep his strength up. What else does Bear like?"

"Redfish with salt, a little pepper. Onions and rosemary."

"Let's go fish, Maddy. I'll take you in my airboat!"

Mister Cochon doesn't adventure as well as Bear. He likes to fiddle. Likes to have the tackle, the fishing poles, the Coleman cooler just so. He drives the airboat put-putter slow, not fast and rollicking like Bear. It's past noon when we reach his favorite fishing spot, far south, near the Gulf waters.

I pinch the bug onto the hook. "Thank you, Bug." Drop my line over the side. Mister Cochon does the same, and we sit and wait and say nothing. That's the best way to fish.

Breathing, watching my line sway, I start to feel better. Maybe Bear can live with Grandmère? Maybe with my family in New Orleans? No, Bear wouldn't like that. He'd be too cooped up in a city without wild animals, wild bushes, and trees.

"What's that, Mister Cochon?"

"Bunch of mud."

"It's moving!"

Mister Cochon steers next to the submerged log and the wiggling mud. "My word, it's a pelican." He cuts the engine. One hand holding tight to the steering wheel, he leans sideways, his thick hand scooping the bird.

"Here, it's slippery."

The pelican, black with oil, is in my lap. It's squirming, scared, trying to get away. But its wings don't flap and its body slips and slides.

"Hold tight, Maddy. Needs help. Else it'll die." Mister Cochon turns the key. The airboat fan roars. Mister Cochon is speeding faster than Bear ever did.

I pat-pat the bird. Oil stains my hand, a thick, sticky seal. The smell makes me nauseous. Limp, the bird's head hangs off my lap. It's still breathing.

"Hold on!" I shout, hoping Pelican can hear above the fan's roar.

We reach the Bon Temps dock. Oil is all over me. I cradle the tiny head. Gripping me by the elbows, Mister Cochon helps me and the pelican down. "Come on, Maddy."

Something makes me look back.

Mami Wata's head is sticking out the water. Her expression scares me.

I run down the path, holding the pelican close to my heart.

I pass Mister Cochon, who's too short-legged and plump to run as fast as me.

"Old Jake, Maddy. Take the bird to Old Jake."

"Jake, help. Help!" Everyone hears me shouting. Jolene stops sewing on the porch. Ben and Charlotte run beside me, keeping pace. "What is it? What is it?" they ask. "What you got?"

I can't stop. I run up Jake's porch steps. The door

opens. "Who's hollering?" His gaze drops to the bird. "Bring her in."

I step inside. There are injured birds in cages—a chicken, a heron, another brown pelican. Diagrams, pictures of Louisiana birds on every surface of the wall.

"Here," he says, clearing an aluminum counter. He turns on a high-powered lamp.

I gently lay down the bird.

Jake winces. "Not sure I can fix this."

"You have to!"

Jake doesn't look at me. With a soft white cloth, he starts to wipe the bird. One cloth, two, twelve pieces of cloth...all of them stained, soaked with crude. You can't tell the pelican used to be brown.

A small yellow eye watches Old Jake. Like the bird knows he's trying to help.

"Get me a bowl of water. Put some Dawn in it."

"Dawn, the dish soap?"

"Helps dissolve the oil. Need to dissolve it, else this pelican dies. May die anyway from the fumes. Or from swallowing crude."

I grab a bowl, fill it with soapy water. Gently, Jake puts the bird in the bowl like it's a baby's bubble bath.

"Ooooh, now, now. Gonna be all right. Ooooh, now, now," Jake keeps repeating. The bird keeps still as Jake washes his feathers. Jake sounds like a bird himself.

In an empty cage, I layer hay and cotton. Jake lays the pelican ever so gently—first its legs, then its body and head.

"Keep warm, Mister Pelican," I say. "Keep warm." The bird sighs, its chest rising and falling, then lies ever so still.

"Now we wait."

"Wait for what?"

"Whether it lives. It's young, still has white plumes on its chest. Did you know pelicans live for thirty years?"

The other caged birds watch the pelican. Like they know he's the sickest one. The pelican's eyes are closed. Jake and I sit, hoping the bird is just sleeping, watching for the rise and fall of its chest.

"What's happening?" I ask, but I already know the answer.

"Oil spill. The deepwater rig is gushing oil."

"Can it be stopped?"

"Nobody knows."

Dreaming True

I dreamed true. Blackness is coloring the water. Crude gushes and stains.

"The well is miles and miles down," I remember Bailey saying. Relentless, crude keeps bubbling, gushing, spreading thousands upon thousands of gallons.

On shore, everyone helps. Even Bear. "Your pa would be proud," I say.

We work hard to save the pelicans.

It takes nearly an hour to clean just one. Every

feather needs to be de-oiled. Every bucket emptied and filled again with clean water and soap.

In a red wagon, Ben and Charlotte keep bringing more oil-soaked pelicans, barely moving. Piles are near my feet. I can't keep up. Bear can't keep up.

The first pelican, recovering in Old Jake's house, didn't live. Jake says oil must've gotten in its lungs.

We keep working on birds as others try to save stranded fish, quickly wiping them clean, then throwing them back into the water. Nobody knows whether they live or die.

Mounds of slick black seaweed and kelp wash ashore. The sand is almost black, smelling like gas.

Downshore, Willie Mae screams. "No, don't come. Don't come!" Her palm is flat, upraised. "Stop, don't let the children come."

Everybody comes. Ben stares. Charlotte cries. Willie Mae picks up Douglass, her body blocking his view.

A dolphin, dead, covered in oil.

Angry, grown-ups shout: "Not right." "Have mercy." "Pitiful, a beautiful animal gone."

I clasp Bear's hand.

A boat horn blares. Blares again. Everyone stops. Some shade their eyes against the sun.

It's Bolden's shrimp boat, with its nets empty, locked high.

The engine growls and Bolden steers the boat straight toward the Bon Temps cove.

Mister Cochon yells, "What's it like out there?"

Bolden's hunched over the helm.

Neighbors gather—Liza, André, Pete. Ben hollers, "Pa, there's a dead dolphin. A big one. Maybe a momma dolphin." Willie Mae pulls him close against her.

Bolden straightens and looks at us, one by one. Then, I think he looks straight at me.

"Oil is spreading fast. Getting closer to Bon Temps. Heard on the radio, the oil company can't cap the well. Nothing's worked."

~

In school, I made a papier-mâché volcano. Soda, a base, and vinegar, an acid, mixed caused fake lava to bubble and explode. For ten seconds, gray foam slithered down my painted volcano's sides.

Miss Avril said, "Real volcanoes can erupt, drain in an hour. But one has been erupting for twenty-four hundred years. Others take twenty years. Most stop erupting after seven weeks."

Though I can't see the seafloor, I imagine it's like a volcano erupting. How long before it stops? It's been days so far. Will it stop spewing in weeks? A month? A year?

I think the crude is alive. It's like slime in black-and-white science fiction movies that gobbles anything in its path. Crude spreads. Strange, in daylight, the slick sheen makes rainbows.

The pelican on my lap has died. Its head hangs backward at an odd angle. I'd almost finished cleaning its feathers, but it didn't matter.

~

Ten days. The oil well still isn't capped.

Today's my birthday. There's no party. No cake. I don't mind.

Ten means change, energy, luck. It's a sign. Maybe, today, the oil well will be capped.

I wait and hope.

~○

Twenty days. There isn't a single hour when someone isn't working. Out at sea, the oil company is still trying to quiet the well. Onshore, Bon Temps folks work. Scientists and students from Dillard and Tulane work, testing the water, cleaning sand, and hauling away rotting plants and dead pelicans, turtles, and dolphins.

Everyone wears masks. A white cup covers my nose and mouth. I breathe funny. Talk funny. But the smell isn't as bad. I don't feel sick as often.

~○

Another pelican has died. I tried not to cry. But it was a baby bird. The whole time I cleaned it, I whispered tales about Sweet Pea and her wandering chicks.

*　　*　　*

I hear the airboat roaring, spinning in the cove. When it stops, Bolden, Mister Cochon, and Pete start unloading sandbags.

Lifting, pushing, pulling the heavy bags, they're trying to build a barrier at the mouth where the Bon Temps tributary reaches the Gulf.

I don't understand. Bon Temps waters are clear. "Mister Cochon." I wave. All three men look at me, their eyes fixed. They're trying too hard not to blink.

"What's it mean, Bear?"

Dull-eyed, he looks at me. "Bon Temps might die."

That can't be my story's end. I won't let it be.

Breathing hurts. I hug my legs, trying to comfort me. Why don't I know what to do? Why didn't I know that Bon Temps's worst hard time hadn't come?

In another few days, another week...I don't want to think about it.

I shut my eyes, but I can't stop seeing the future.

Crude is in the inlets and cove, spoiling waterways, killing life. Ruining Bayou Bon Temps.

I don't want to think about it. I *have* to think about it. This is what I was getting ready for—saving Bon Temps.

Another Dream

Bear snores, whimpers in his sleep. On the porch, I lie on my side, trying to dream on purpose. It's hard. I breathe slow. Squeeze my eyes. Toss and turn. Punch my pillow.

I roll on my back. Relax, I tell myself. Breathe.

I'm ready, I tell myself.

It matters that this was my year to have a bayou summer. I've been getting ready to keep Bon Temps alive.

But I don't know how.

I exhale, punch the pillow, and turn on my side.

The bayou is quiet, like all the animals, worried, have run away. Not even an owl hoots. The weeping willows' branches seem lower, sweeping the ground.

Time is running out. Sunday, Ma will come to take me home.

I sniff, wipe my eyes. My firefly lands on the porch right in front of me. Hope is so tiny—little feet, delicate wings, black beady eyes. Her stomach glows—blinking, on then off, on then off. Her blinking slows.

I focus on her light. I see pictures.

Poisonous crude gushes, spreading outward in all directions, cloaking the blue-green sea. It travels with the currents, lapping onward, trying to reach shore. Hundreds of ocean miles are spoiled.

I see me—onshore, arms and hands beckoning. I'm calling someone. I can't see who. Mami Wata?

Then I hear, "Build it. Make it strong."

Now I'm tumbling, falling through water. I'm in the Bon Temps swamp.

I hear again, "Build it. Make it strong." It's me. I'm the one speaking.

Then I see mermaids, hundreds of them, pushing, moving mud, rock, and silt. From the bottom of the swamp, they're building a levee. A huge dam to block the river's mouth.

I wake up. Hope hasn't moved. She still glows.

I finally know...I know how my story ends. With courage and hope. "Right, Hope?" I ask.

I slip on my tennis shoes. Bear stirs but doesn't wake. Once beyond Grandmère's yard, I run.

"Come, fireflies. Come." And they do—maybe Hope's entire kin. Thousands of fireflies, more than I've ever seen before, lighting my path.

This Is How It Ends

I stand at the swamp's edge. The world is green and hushed. Broken logs stick half in and half out of the water. Gators float, their bulging eyes just above water. A beaver scurries, dragging a branch.

"Mami Wata." All the fireflies hover behind me.

"Mami Wata, please come."

Mami Wata surfaces and swims close. Staring into her eyes, I see me. I see Membe chained in a ship's hold. I see Grandmère.

"You've always been here," I say. "Thank you."

Pleased, Mami Wata nods. I hear bell-like sounds.

I speak slowly, trying to get my words right. "You left your home to support Membe, my family. Even when they stopped believing in you, when they didn't have enough imagination to see you, you've been here. Believing in them."

Wata lifts her tail, water streaming like a waterfall.

"Oil is spilling in the Gulf. An unbelievable amount of oil, and it's ruining everything.

"I don't want to lose Bon Temps, Mami Wata. Don't want Grandmère, Mister Cochon, Bolden and Willie Mae's family, or anyone else to get hurt. Don't want to lose animals, rabbits, fish, and birds. Or sassafras, flowers, and cypress."

Angry, Mami Wata shakes, slaps her tail.

"Yes, not a bit of it, Mami Wata. None of it should be hurt. But it is hurting—being harmed right now in the Gulf of Mexico. We can't save the whole Gulf. Just like we can't stop an oil volcano. But we can save Bon Temps. Build a levee. A levee so strong, it keeps the oil from getting in, from ruining our home."

Mami Wata watches me, her face serious. *A young face with strength*, I think. Like me.

"I've been getting ready," I declare, standing tall. "To save Bon Temps. We need a happier ending."

I raise my hands high. "Fireflies, come." Tiny lights swirl over and above my palms. "We must ask Mami Wata for help."

The fireflies swarm Mami Wata, their lights sparkling, making her appear more beautiful. My firefly, Hope, rests on her shoulder while the others make patterns more beautiful than stars.

"I think there were more mermaids like you. More who followed slave ships to new worlds. More who loved children, and maybe not just children, but any kidnapped soul."

Wata's head tilts. Moonlight glows.

I feel both sorrow and happiness. "Call them, Mami Wata. Ask them to help us build a levee. To save Bon Temps. Please. Pretty, pretty please, Mami Wata."

Mami Wata dives and, though she doesn't ask, I dive, too.

The water is so warm. I float on my back. Fireflies dance.

I hear a loud, resonating sound, an urgent call rippling high-pitched through the waters. I hear it again. Currents quicken; fish scatter.

Mami Wata surfaces beside me. I flip over and we dive deep. She's smiling. I know exactly what she's going to do. She blows a trail of bubbles. I swallow them, breathing underwater.

We swim south. I let Mami Wata pull me along, since her tail is so powerful. We glide swift like dolphins. Every few miles, she stops and calls out again. *"Sisters, kin, come."*

We swim on, and above us, the fireflies keep us company.

Fresh swamp water is mixing with ocean salt. This is the river's mouth.

"Sisters, kin, come."

Quiet, we surface, treading water and searching the horizon.

Long stretches of slick crude cover huge patches of ocean like scabs.

Mami Wata stares and stares, and I *feel* more than ever that she's ancient, other, and though she doesn't cry or say a word, I *feel* such sadness, much larger, deeper than Grandmère or any other human could bear.

I hear a whistling sound. Then, another voice. A call, maybe? Some kind of shout. Mami Wata smiles.

"Oh, my," I breathe. Mermaids, dozens and dozens, are swimming toward us. I recognize the white-haired mermaid. The mermaid with silver scales and black eyes. There are all kinds of mermaids—with faces mirroring different ages—young like me, old like Ma and Pa, older like Grandmère, and a couple who seem beyond old, with nearly translucent skin.

"They're all beautiful," I say. Silver, purple, black, and gray scales. Tails that arch, slap and make them glide, skim, leap across waves. White hair, black hair, and chestnut brown. Some lips are blue, some pink, some red, and some just brown.

Mami Wata talks without speaking.

Hundreds of mermaids agree to save Bon Temps. Agree, in unison, to dive, swift down to the river bottom to push mud, rock, and silt. To build a levee from the bottom up.

They listened. They will do what I dreamed.

Because of me, there is a happy end.

My Story

Ma hugs Grandmère for so long I start to fidget. Then she gets in the car and we start the drive back to New Orleans. To my other home.

The bayou starts to fade into paved roads, traffic signs, cars and trucks going places.

After a hundred miles, we get to the main road. Ma turns on the radio.

First it's mostly static, then we hear:

"They're calling it the Bon Temps miracle. The oil has parted around this bayou like the eye of a hurricane. Scientists are stumped. Seabirds are flocking to the clear coastline, plants are staying green, the water clear. Here's Thomas Bolden, a local shrimper. 'Even the shrimp are fine. Bon Temps is famous for its shrimp.'"

I smile and silently thank Mami Wata.

Ma says, "That's amazing. How lucky for Bon Temps. I was so worried about the spill."

"It wasn't luck, Ma."

"No?"

"I'll tell you the story, but you have to promise me one thing."

"What?"

"I get to spend every summer in Bon Temps with Grandmère, Bear, and my other friends."

Ma laughs. "Of course you can, Maddy."

"Well, then, this is my story."

Ma listens quiet.

"Oh, my," she says, reaching across the seat and squeezing my hand. "You're a hero."

I don't say anything.

In real life, it's hard to be a hero. Bad things

happen and you can't fix everything yourself. You need good friends and hope. Sometimes, even mermaids.

I look right, out the window. It's getting dark. We're approaching New Orleans—more concrete and fewer trees. Tall buildings and harsh shadows.

I whisper, calling, "Come, fireflies."

I exhale. Tiny lights flit low among bushes, dotting the horizon, blinking warmly at me.

I imagine Grandmère on her porch, waiting for me, waiting for our next summer.

A Note from the Author

I've always loved Louisiana—its people, culture, and landscape. I'd just finished writing *Ninth Ward*, a novel about the human and environmental disasters caused by Hurricane Katrina and the levees breaking. To my horror, the evening news was filled with images of the Deepwater Horizon oil rig explosion— flames leaping, fireboats spraying water, plumes of black smoke, and crude oil spreading over the Gulf waters. Eleven rig workers died in the explosion, and more than two hundred million gallons of crude polluted the environment. To date, the Deepwater Horizon spill is the worst oil disaster in US history.

In *Bayou Magic*, my heroine, Maddy, uses her

intelligence and magical powers to rescue her community from environmental catastrophe.

Maddy is a symbol of hope and my personal praise song for all the young people who care about being good stewards of our air, land, and water, and the earth's natural resources.

Louisiana, in particular, has always been subject to severe weather and environmental damage. Natural disasters are unavoidable, but human-caused disasters may be more easily averted if we learn from the past. You, dear reader, and your generation will have the ongoing challenge of balancing the use of natural resources with safety for humans, animals, and the planet.

For me, the legend of Mami Wata was a perfect counterpoint to the oil spill. Mami Wata, "Mother Water," was the name given to African water spirits in the pidgin English used by slave traders. There are countless folktale variations regarding the spiritual powers and gifts of half-fish, half-human Mami Wata.

Mermaid legends abound throughout all cultures. For me, this tale spoke of such love, loyalty, and community. Symbolically, too, it affirmed the cultural contributions, present and future, that Africans would make to American culture.

In a time of need—to save the Bon Temps community and its environment—Maddy calls upon the grace of mermaids, her spiritual ancestors.

In Maddy, I poured all my love for young people who seek, each and every day, new and better ways to care for our earth.

Sincerely,

Jewell

Acknowledgments

Deep thanks to Liza Baker, executive editorial director at Little, Brown Books for Young Readers. Your professionalism, challenging critiques, and support always inspired me. Special thanks, too, to Allison Moore, assistant editor, who also guided and supported me and helped bring Madison Isabelle Lavalier Johnson to life.

Thank you, thank you to Mollie Connelly, my Arizona State University research assistant (and future librarian).

Love to my husband, Brad, who always encourages me. Thank you for bringing Ripley and Gurgi, our two Australian shepherds, into our lives. Ripley and Gurgi brought me joy and kept me company while I wrote. They already knew that mermaids existed.